W9-AAH-111

Mother Superior

Mother Superior

Stories

Saleema Nawaz

Copyright © 2008 by Saleema Nawaz

All rights reserved. No part of this publication may be reproduced, stored in a
retrieval system, or transmitted in any form or by any means graphic, electronic, or
mechanical—including photocopying, recording, and taping—without prior written
permission of the publisher, or, in the case of photocopying or other reprographic
copying, a license from the Canadian Copyright Licensing Agency (Access
Copyright), One Yonge Street, Suite 1900, Toronto, ON, Canada, M5E 1E5.

Library and Archives Canada Cataloguing in Publication

Nawaz, Saleema, 1979-

    Mother Superior : stories / Saleema Nawaz.

ISBN 978-1-55111-927-4

    I.Title.

PS8627.a94M68 2008   C813'.6   C2008-90356-4

Freehand Books
412 – 815 1st St SW
Calgary, Alberta
Canada T2P 1N3
www.freehand-books.com

Book orders
Broadview Press Inc.
280 Perry Street, Unit 5
Peterborough, Ontario
Canada K9J 7H5
phone: 705-743-8990
fax: 705-743-8353
customerservice@broadviewpress.com
www.broadviewpress.com

Printed in Canada

Freehand Books, an imprint of Broadview Press Inc., acknowledges the financial
support for its publishing program provided by the Government of Canada though
the Book Publishing Industry Development Program (BPIDP).

BLUE MOUNTAINS CITY LIBRARY

20.1.09.

52 16 7176368

NAWAZ

Table of Contents

Mother Superior

JOAN WON'T GET AN ABORTION. She says she is a slut but
a slut for Jesus. She doesn't go to church but chugs cases
of Baby Duck and calls it communion wine. She wipes
her mouth with the back of her hand, says it won't hurt
the baby. At worst, she says, it might make it slow. The
kind of kid who could never leave you.

A little less likely to see the evil in the world is how
she finally puts it.

Joan used to think that I would go to hell for being a
lesbian, but now she thinks I'll make it to purgatory because I'm practically a nun anyway. This makes me think
that our house is like a home for unwed mothers. Joan is
a wayward girl, I'm Mother Superior, and when the baby is

ready to come out someone will take it away forever. Then it will be just the two of us.

Gerard, the seed of the miracle, is in Thompson. He has no idea of Joan's last name or of what has sprouted up in this southern city since his sudden departure. Joan says she thinks Gerard is a miner, toiling in the belly of the north, blasting riches from the dirt with his strong arms and shoulders. But I think of him as a pirate, working the shaft only to conceal his treasure, planting jewels in the walls of the earth. I think Joan must be marked with an X in a spot I can't see, and I find myself watching for Gerard, expecting him to return to claim his cache.

IT IS SPRING AND SHE WALKS to meet me every day after work, bored by then of the soap operas she watches during the afternoon. It is the first time in her life since junior high that she has stopped working, and she claims it agrees with her. She says nobody wants to see a pregnant waitress while they're eating, as though the gentle bulge on her slight frame might put them off their coleslaw.

By the time we get inside, Joan is tired from the spurt of exercise, her body fueled only by cigarettes, alcohol, and junk food. I try to picture the baby in her belly, twisting on its cord, stunted by the poisons in her system. It's hard for me to believe in something I can't see, which is maybe why Joan believes in God and I don't. But even she doesn't seem to believe in this yet, the tiny thief without a face living as a parasite off her blood.

She kicks off her flip-flops. The space between her first two toes is split, oozing wet and pink. I look for Band-aids as she lowers herself onto the corduroy couch.

"Why do you wear them if they hurt your feet?" I ask. The medicine cabinet is a test pattern of a drugstore advertisement. Scooby-Doo Band-aids nestled between Imodium tablets and Revlon shimmer powder.

Joan stares at the ceiling. "Why do women have babies if it feels like their insides are being ripped out?"

Before I reply she adds, "None of my other shoes will fit around my ankles anymore."

SHE IS BLARING THE STEREO AS LOUD as it will go, so loud the framed Spanish devotional cards are vibrating. The saints hold their tongues, and so do I, thinking about the instincts of animals, the laws of nature that force us all to make our own mistakes. Cradling her belly, Joan bangs her head to the rhythm, pressing her stomach up against the black of the speaker. Her face lost in the grease and tangle of her hair.

"I want to blow its fucking ears out," she screams over the music. "I don't ever want to hear it whining it wants to go to Disneyworld."

It turns out that babies can hear in the womb, their tiny fishbone ears as sensitive as telephone wires. Joan says she'll teach it sign language and their house will be silent and peaceful as a church. There will be only coughing and the drawing of breaths. The almost inaudible noises of waiting and growing.

IN THE SUMMER SHE IS HUGE and dating a guy named Larry, a thin, tenuous man with pleated pants. He keeps one hand on Joan's arm as she introduces him. I notice his bony wrists, the darkened sacs under his eyes. I see Joan push back her shoulders, touch one finger to the gloss on her bottom lip. She's wearing perfume again, the scent of jasmine and oranges reminding me of Gerard and every other guy, every other time I could feel myself pulling away.

He is explaining how they met. Her leaving the video store, green and yellow cotton stretched over her basketball stomach, beads of sweat on her forehead and between her bare shoulder blades. Him walking down Portage, alive to beauty, seeing only the freshness of youthful bodies and the Saturday high heels, saying no to all the people asking for change and then following her into Tim Hortons because he is impulsive and believes in taking control of his own destiny. His bottom lip juts out, pulls to the right as he says the word, and I think of asking him to say fate, kismet, providence to see if the smirk is a congenital tic or rather a revelation of his own skepticism.

Larry believes in the purity of the sexual impulse. He tells me he knew when he started following Joan that she would not be wearing a wedding band.

"Sometimes, it's true, they're not wearing them because their fingers have become too swollen, but more often than not, married women will give off a different vibe. They have this kind of insular aura of self-satisfaction, which is in itself very sexy. But Joanie was giving off this extremely intense current of almost primordial vigour. I could tell that she felt powerful and that her sense of power was making her aroused."

Joan smiles, stirs her chamomile tea with a chopstick. Behind Larry's back, she winks at me, grabbing her own breast. My spine relaxes and I grin back. Then Larry is a brownish blur as I focus on her face, wishing for this to really be a convent after all, with Larry outside at the door, begging for sanctuary.

At first Larry thinks I'm interesting. He asks what I know about dildos, clit rings, and fisting. I ask him what he knows about print pornography and little boys.

Frowns wrinkle Larry's forehead. He pushes his hair behind his ears.

"I am not a pedophile or any kind of pervert. I am a connoisseur of a rare beauty."

Larry refuses to allow his pride to be wounded by the oddity of his sexuality. He calls me a prudish dyke, then a dykish prude because he says I am more uptight than anything else.

IT IS JOAN'S BIRTHDAY, and I give her a feather boa—pink, flecked with threads of gold. Larry nods, licks his lips in approval. He says it is traditional to give a striptease when presented with the gift of a boa. I tell him he is full of shit and Joan laughs, her muscular face in sudden contrast to the soft pliancy of her body at rest. She struggles off the couch, puts James Taylor on the stereo. The boa droops from her neck, falling to either side of her breasts. Joan steps to the hooked rug at the foot of the couch and plants herself in the centre, the dark, bloated surfaces of her feet crisscrossed with sharp, pale lines of untanned skin.

Eyes closing, Joan pulls at the sides of her flowered

sundress. I see her calves, the hair rubbed away on the insides of her legs.

"I love a woman who doesn't shave," Larry confides. His mouth is straight and serious. I look at him watching her, at the hollow of his eyes under his brow, and I pray that my desire is less obvious. My goal is to be as selfless as a surrogate, to love and to claim nothing. Even Joan's absent-father of a deity, that perfect model of non-interference, requires more.

Joan giggles, dropping to her knees. Her fingers find her hair, twisting out the tangles that have grown in the dark, matting at the back of her skull during her long hours on the couch. I lower myself to the floor and, thrusting my hand in, I feel the stickiness of her hair between my fingers, the feverish warmth of her scalp. I draw down my hand, coaxing out the snarls.

"Let me wash your hair," I say.

I twist open the taps, pouring in capfuls of raspberry-scented bubble bath. She asks me to light eight of the nine Our Lady of Guadalupe candles that line the window ledge and I do, using the long wooden matches from the jar beside them. Resting one hand on her stomach, Joan tests the running water, her knees pressing against the wide, curving edge of the claw-footed tub. She tells me that temperatures over 38 degrees have been linked to birth defects, and, stooping, she adds more cold water. She catches me looking at her, her face an amused mirror of my own surprise and relief. And I grin back, blinking too rapidly, my cheeks hot and flushed.

Joan's robe falls from her shoulders and I hold her hand as she steps into the tub. Tiny blue spider veins blossom across the roundness of her stretched skin. Below the trailing edge of her hair, her breasts are heavy and large, twice the size they were in the winter. I feel my nipples harden as I look at hers, the dark pink buds that make smacking sounds in Larry's mouth when he sucks on them. And then she is in, slick beneath the frothy blanket of bubbles.

I bring down the showerhead to wash her hair, and when I am done, she turns it on me, soaking my baggy clothes with the spray until they cling, until I peel them off and leap into the water. Toe to shoulder, shoulder to toe, we prune ourselves in the tub until the bubbles have all disappeared.

IT IS SEPTEMBER AND WE ARE HANGING the photo above the fireplace. Joan nude and resplendently pregnant, a three-quarter profile in a golden glow. Larry is more modest than I expect and I compliment him on his work.

"It doesn't take any talent to make that look beautiful," he says, and Joan smiles. I look from her open face and loose dark hair to Larry's patterned purple shirt and scuffed loafers.

"I bet you have a big photo collection on your computer, eh, Larry?"

He looks at me, scratches in a vague way at the hair on his chest.

"Yes I do. Almost three thousand. Only a small percentage is my own work, however."

There is nothing for me to say then, for Joan's water breaks and Larry's face falls as he begins to weep.

THE TAXI WEAVES THROUGH HEAVY TRAFFIC toward the hospital. The taxi driver explains that he is taking his time because he used to be a doctor in his own country. Joan tells him that she needs drugs, that otherwise she would be happy to have him deliver her baby. The taxi driver nods, looking back at us in his rear-view mirror. Larry sits on his right, staring straight ahead. Joan's cries of pain remind me of the sounds of her sex with Larry, the small yelps I always imagined to be coming from the baby within.

At the entrance to the hospital, I find a wheelchair and help Joan from the taxi, my hands shaking in time to her quick, shallow breaths. Larry is tender, regretful. He bends to kiss Joan's belly, his skinny fingers running down toward her crotch. His hand planted between her legs, he fixes his eyes on her flushed, contorted face.

"You are so hot," he says, and leaves. He gets into the back seat that we've just vacated, waving aside the confusion of the driver. I tell Joan he is probably sniffing the upholstery for one last kick, and she grabs my hand, pulling me now, tugging me down close to beg me to hurry.

My Three Girls

THERE IS A PHOTOGRAPH OF ME AND KATHLEEN in the rec room with Maggie, our dead baby sister. She is slumped in a car seat, swaddled in a pink flannel blanket, eyes and mouth sutured shut, every crease turned down with the heaviness of death. Kathleen and I are posed to either side, legs outstretched, hips pressed into the orange carpet. We have our chins in our hands, and Kathleen has one bare foot kicked up in the air. A couple of half-dressed Barbie dolls are visible off in the corner. A picnic-pose photo, like the one of us in Stanley Park, the checkered print of our two matching sundresses vivid against the striped grey blanket, our island in the sea of green grass.

In the Stanley Park photo, our faces are bright, our smiles wide and eager. Kathleen is grinning, her eyes flirting with the camera as though she could bewitch it with a direct gaze. The same sly but alluring look I can trace through all the family photos, from her class pictures to her wedding scrapbook. Behind us is a patch of blue, Lost Lagoon winking in the sun. When I look at myself half-squinting, I can remember the breeze coming off the water and our father's indulgence in buying us swirled candy sticks on the way to the bus stop. Jockeying with Kathleen for the window seat until the end of my tutti-frutti stick got tangled up in her blonde hair. A lingering, luminous day.

In the photo with Maggie, we are smiling, too, but the effect is disturbing. Our charms are displayed to better advantage by the closer angle, and beautiful Kathleen, at seven, is radiant against the drab wood panelling of our finished basement. Her smile, so beguiling and intense, barely eclipses my own here, for in this photo I actually seem to be giggling, betraying my crooked teeth as my brown ponytail flails forward in a messy signal of movement. I can barely pick out the rims of the glasses I used to hate, and I seem at home in my eleven-year-old body, unselfconscious about the exposed roll of stomach bulging in a pale band from under my purple T-shirt. The girth of my hips already large enough, as I lie lengthwise, to dwarf the car seat that is set before us.

I cannot imagine what we could have been thinking, though it is likely that it was our mother who told us to smile. In her album, this photo is captioned "My Three Girls."

WHEN MY HUSBAND TELLS ME he doesn't want us to get a midwife, he invokes Maggie as a reason for going to the hospital. He thinks he is at his most persuasive after dinner, when I am full and tired and tend to agree with anything.

"But your baby sister, though. I thought your mother— well, am I right in thinking that your mother had her at home?"

The hesitation in his question irks me, although I know it is only his attempt at tact, at not venturing to express more than I would presume him to feel. He knows the circumstances of Maggie's death as well as anyone in the family. As well as anyone might, having met my mother even once.

"Maggie didn't die because she was born at home," I say. "She died because she had a birth defect that would have killed her no matter where she was born."

I remember my father, dry-eyed and harried, explaining how what had happened to Maggie was not quite as sad as if she could have lived but had died anyway. "It is a tragedy, yes," he said, the side of his mouth sagging open as Kathleen and I gawked. "A tragedy has befallen this family. But it is something closer to a disappointment than a devastation." This, though our mother's noisy weeping kept on unabated from behind their bedroom door.

"Oh." Eric turns away for a moment, stooping under the sink for dish soap, before attempting, "But what does your mother think?"

Which is his way of saying that my mother won't like it and that, by even considering a home birth, we're signing ourselves up for weeks of her heartrending pleas—speeches that will make me mourn my sister, and the woman my mother used to be, and the way I was once able to feel grief and pity and know that they were in no way mixed with apathy or contempt.

→

UNTIL KATHLEEN WAS BORN, I had never liked dolls. Their puckered lips and grappling fingers were nothing to me compared to the soft snout of a teddy bear or the fluffy tail of a stuffed cat.

Kathleen was squishy like a plush animal and warm besides. I was captivated by her multitude of tiny expressions, sometimes even poking her in the side with my index finger to see a ripple of unhappiness clench her amazing, volatile face. I wondered how we had ever lived without her, without someone who could take us away from ourselves and the petty tedium of whatever had consumed us before.

When they brought Maggie home for the wake, she reminded me of those old dolls, as light as if she were filled only with air instead of with tiny muscles and bones and her still, imperfect heart. She was hard, too, like the dolls, except for her feet, which were soft and movable. My mother told us it was because the veins there were too tiny to be embalmed, and Kathleen stroked the soles of them with one finger, crooning "Cootchie-cootchie-coo" until my mother slapped her hand away and took Maggie upstairs to be passed around among the guests.

ERIC IS INCREDULOUS that my mother still hasn't seen our baby in anything besides the dozens of snapshots taken by Kathleen.

"Your daughter has a baby, you go," he says. I smile at him because I find his indignation, when it is on my behalf, charming. His bottom lip juts out as his head begins a concise quiver of disapproval, his hands rubbing up and down against the small of his back in a flap-wing posture of concern. My hand on his cheek stops him, and he leans into my touch before shrugging his shoulders. He collapses into the chair beside Ava's crib, the one that provides the best vantage point for parental doting and gloating. "My mother has been practically living here for the past four weeks," he says.

"I know." Laundered little outfits are folded neatly in piles near the changing table, and prepared meals are stacked deep into the freezer, their mottled surfaces speckled with frost like snow-capped peaks. "She's been a big help."

"Well, then. Doesn't your mother care at all?"

And because there is no answer to this question that he will understand, I tell him I will call her and invite myself over.

MY MOTHER PACES THE KITCHEN, drying dishes, stirring the soup, following a nervous course around the perimeter of the table where I am sitting with the baby. Ava fusses in a way that is unusual for her, her mouth falling open in an impression of wild anguish. As I soothe her, I imagine she senses my mother's nervous energy, her inability to comprehend good news.

Despite my father's best rallying attempts, my parents' circle narrowed with Maggie's death, whittled down to relatives and those with a taste or tolerance for grief. Even now, with the evidence of a healthy baby right before her, my mother's interest is on Ava's narrow escape.

"So are you in a lot of pain?" she asks. She nods with sympathy toward my belly, which beneath my shirt is now scarred in a red and glistening line from the surgery.

"A little." My mother's predictions of calamity have stifled certain aspects of our conversations. When, during my third trimester, I confided that I hadn't felt the baby move in a day and a half, she surmised aloud that the baby was probably dead. She looked huffy and bewildered when Eric, arriving to pick me up, gave her only a curt hello before helping me out to the car.

My mother begins scrubbing new potatoes in the colander. She looks over at me from the sink. "You ought to have tried to lose some of that weight before having a baby," she says. "It isn't healthy."

"That's true." I raise my eyebrows at her before looking down to stroke the side of Ava's cheek, watching her cries quiet down as her exhaustion takes over. "Remind me to give you your clothes back as soon as I start to drop some of these pounds."

"Oh, you." My mother shakes her head and brings the washed potatoes and a peeler to the counter nearest to the table. "It's true, you know. You shouldn't be like me."

My mother is drawing closer to Ava bit by bit. She grabs a handful of potato peels and steps toward the garbage can to the right of the table. On her way, I see her shoot a glance at the baby, her pupils dilating until her brown eyes are suffused in black.

"Why don't you sit down?" I kick with my foot at the chair opposite me until it budges out from the table. Its clatter against the linoleum makes Ava open her eyes and give a small, plaintive cry.

My mother throws the peels in the garbage and settles on the chair, clucking her disapproval.

"Honestly, you should know better," she says. "Give her here. I'll quiet her."

And so I hand her the baby, and she takes her from me with strong, sure hands, her lips moving with the start of a lullaby.

IN BED AT NIGHT, WE PRETENDED MAGGIE was a ghost who was watching us. Not an angel, because it didn't seem possible that she could wish us well. Not after we had seen her in her grim final repose.

"If you don't get up and close that closet door," I said, "Maggie will try and choke you to death in your sleep."

"Why would she try and do that?" Kathleen's voice was piteous with a rehearsed tremulousness of fear. The conversation was a kind of game we liked to play.

"Because she's jealous of us. Because we're alive and she isn't. Because she knows we're happy that she's gone."

"I'm not," said Kathleen.

"Yes, you are. You're happy because if she was alive you wouldn't be able to take ballet lessons because we wouldn't have enough money." I didn't know if this was true, but it struck me as a brilliant inspiration.

"Really?" There was a rustling in the darkness as Kathleen half-sat up in her bed.

"Really. And she knows you think she's ugly. She knows you told me that you thought she looked weird." Another inspiration on my roll of cruelty. In the confused weeks after the funeral, Kathleen had confided to me that she thought Maggie didn't look like a normal baby. "She was a funny colour," she'd whispered, as our mother arranged a tiny framed photo of Maggie on the centre of the mantelpiece behind a white tea light. Maggie's mottled face was patchy purple and red from the poor breathing that never even really got started.

"How does Maggie know that?" asked Kathleen, who by now was fully sitting up. I could see the shadow her rumpled hair cast against the wall by the glow of our snowflake nightlight. "Will she tell Mummy?"

"No," I said, and my shoulders shook in a sudden quake as I pictured a bundled Maggie hovering near my mother's sleeping face. Sometimes I scared even myself in these late-night chats. "No, I don't think so."

→

IN THE WAITING ROOM, KATHLEEN LOOKS healthier than the other patients, her hair cut short but grown thicker than ever, and I can see them turning to me, peeking up from the aged magazines to scout my body for the signs of sickness, for a benchmark of suffering against which they can measure their own recovery or decline. I can see the conclusions forming, a speculation of tumours hidden under layers of fat, the oddly defensive attributions of blame upon an obese woman for a disease she must have brought upon herself. Next to my sister, I look like the one who deserves to be struck down.

But if they were to look up from Kathleen's stomach

and its promising bulge, they might notice the boyish plane of her chest, the fierce clenching of the jaw that has tightened her winning smile into the wryest imaginable grin—the only traces of her illness visible since remission.

When she was laid low in the hospital, she claimed she wouldn't miss her breasts, calling them her "bad luck magnets." "What did they ever do for me?" she'd say, sipping water from a paper cup as though it might be a daiquiri or the sangria we used to mix in a bucket when we went to the cabin in the summer. "Besides getting me a couple of bad boyfriends and a loser of an ex-husband?" She'd giggled. Greg was an angel, a formalist poet she divorced when she began sleeping with his brother. After the affair and a couple of aggrieved sonnets, Greg was now her most devoted friend.

"Not to mention cancer."

"Exactly."

My cheeks often ached from our nervy, hysterical laughter behind the curtain of the pink recovery room, and I never looked away because the only thing back then, the only thing that could make Kathleen upset, was for people to look away from her, to drop their gaze from the sight of her skinny, determined face.

✦

THERE ARE OTHER PHOTOS OF MAGGIE. A whole album of them sat on the mantelpiece for a year after her death, until my father removed it to an upstairs closet. It is a small, square album, bound in white leather, with only one photograph per page. Documenting my youngest sister from her conception to her funeral, its first few pages consist of side-profile shots of my mother's pregnant belly covered in a bright floral print almost matching the wallpaper, her stomach like a balloon in high relief. The next six pages hold a series showing Maggie's brief stay in the plastic bassinet of the ICU, tubes obscuring her face and small body. Beneath the fifth photograph taken at the hospital, my mother has written, in her neat and regular handwriting, "This is the last photo of Maggie alive."

Most of the rest are snapshots taken at the wake, with various friends and relatives holding Maggie's embalmed body, their tight and solemn faces barely concealing their horror. The very last photograph in the book is of my parents huddled on the gravesite before the funeral. The tiny white coffin sits ready for burial on the grass before them, projecting a sturdy kind of cheerfulness as it gleams in the sunlight. My father sits cross-legged, his arm around my mother's slumped shoulders. His face is downcast, yet I project upon him an invisible embarrassment, an awareness of the professional photographer who must have staged the tableau of grief.

My father is dead now, too, but there are no photographs of his grave or of the small ceremony attended by our family and a few of his students from the university. He suffered a stroke on his way home from a lecture and died, the next day, without having opened his eyes. When I called Kathleen to tell her to come to the hospital, she was already there for radiation treatment. Our mother, who'd been bracing herself for a different disaster, whispered to me as we pulled up in the cab, "He doesn't want to live to see another child die."

"He didn't do this on purpose," I said, but she was already hurrying inside, the sound of her wheezes and her heavy, uneven footsteps still audible from the pavement.

➔

IT'S OBVIOUS THAT THE DOCTOR is angry at Kathleen. She is clutching her clipboard to her chest, her eyes glancing over at me instead of at my sister. It is the irritability and embarrassment of bad news. The doctor is normally very pleasant.

"We knew that this could happen," she says. "We knew it was a risk."

"I know," says Kathleen.

"This is why we tell people to wait at least two years."

"I know," repeats Kathleen. "I'm not blaming you." She shrugs, and in this oncology office the gesture has a fatalistic bravado that makes my heart sink. "It could have come back anyways, even if I didn't stop taking the drugs."

The doctor is shaking her head, her face severe as she talks about lymph nodes and advanced stages, and Kathleen is nodding. She says, "I don't want to hurt the baby. After she's born I'll do whatever you think is best." She struggles out of the chair with the help of my hand and adds, "If it's worth it."

I had my chance, eight months before this, to talk my sister out of it. She'd taken me aside to tell me she was undergoing tests. She wanted to know whether her eggs were still viable after her treatment.

"When do you get the results back?" I asked, trying not to sound too thrilled, for I had begun to feel superstitious since Kathleen's illness and our father's death. As though Maggie, lonesome and implacable, was still watching us for signs of too much happiness.

Kathleen laughed as she bounced Ava on her knee. "I don't know exactly. It's a kind of self-administered test." She winked at me. "Greg's helping."

—

SOMETIMES WHEN AVA IS QUIET and I am holding her against my body, or when she is strapped into the sling carrier, dozing, I imagine that I am still pregnant, that the cancer that killed my sister is still being held at bay, and that Kathleen is not another tragedy to be added to my mother's litany of sorrow. My breathing slows, and my eyes begin closing until my daughter stirs and I let reality surge back, traces of guilt lapping at the edge of my consciousness. But I don't wish Ava away, only back inside, buffered from my uselessness at keeping people safe.

Setting Ava down on the play mat, I bring Meghan to my breast to be fed, as I did even before her mother passed away. She looks enough like Ava to be her sister, though her features are always changing, her face first looking longer, then rounder. Her blue eyes looking darker, then wiser.

My mother is moving around in the next room, asking aloud how I ever let my bathtub get so filthy, until she drowns herself out by turning on the taps. She stays over during the week now, helping with the house and the babies. But sometimes I catch her looking at me as though she can't understand why she was left with the least promising one, the heavy one that takes life too seriously, the one most like her. And at night, when I get up to check on the babies, each sleeping in a crib in the nursery, I sometimes see my mother walking from room to room, her face sagging in grief, looking like a lost little girl.

Bloodlines

MY SISTER AND I STOPPED BLEEDING at the same time. It was the start of a baby that stopped me, or what my father called my shame before he died of it, keeling over downstairs in our bagel shop. A heart attack, and he fell hard, though his turban cushioned his head as it struck one of the metal trays on the way down. The night shift said it sounded like a gong, which made me think death knell, and they said that uncooked circles of dough were scattered everywhere, one sticking to the ceiling and one smacking Little Carlos in the ear, giving him a case of vertigo that made him nauseous whenever he happened to cross the Jacques Cartier bridge in the daytime.

If I were a different kind of sister, one who wasn't

nosy as hell, it might have taken me longer to find out she wasn't bleeding. But we lived in such close quarters there, in the oven heat of the upper apartment, that we were like animals together in our rhythms and our motions, rising as one beast with the sun and bleeding with the moon.

That was Mama's innovation, making our time coincide with the full moon. She did it by drawing our blinds on all nights except when the moon was full, and on those nights leaving on a nightlight, until our cycles were synched to each other and to the sky. It was something she'd learned when she was a hippie, before she converted to Sikhism and married our father and lived a life with what I imagine to be a normal share of happiness and regrets, though of course there's no way of really knowing.

It was just at the end of our street that she died in a bike accident, hit by the delivery truck bringing us our poppy seeds. This was only a year before my shame began its existence as a tiny fertilized egg, probably no bigger than a poppy seed itself, so I don't blame myself exclusively for my father's heart attack but rather the standard combination of circumstance and bad luck that precipitates most tragedies, a mix of faulty brakes, cholesterol, humidity, God, broken condoms, taxes, and guilt.

I say this mostly because Mama's way was to try and be funny about the bad stuff, to joke about the most awful things that could happen. She said that both times she was pregnant she used to joke to Papa that she was incubating a canary or a Golden Retriever. It made him nervous to hear it, and a little confused, but it made her relieved, and less afraid. But of course it's a bit different in that case because nothing bad had happened to them yet.

IT WAS THE NIGHT BEFORE THE FULL MOON, but the waxing moon hung as round and bright as if looking to refute the almanac and claim the night for itself. We had the bathroom window open, to help with the heat, and my sister, where she was, would have been able to see the moon's reflection in the gold-flecked mirror of the medicine cabinet as I rummaged through all three shelves with one hand, pretending to look. It knew it was our day to start, and I knew by this time what was wrong with me, and being an elaborate sort of liar rather than a liar by omission I took out one crisply wrapped tampon for myself and passed one to my sister.

"Care to de-virginize yourself again?" I asked. This was in reference to our father's fury when he discovered we were using tampons rather than pads. He wouldn't say the words but warned that we were going to ruin ourselves. Our mother, telling us over her shoulder that we had to use the natural, unbleached cotton kind, smoothed his black beard with her left hand, calling him an old fool before kissing him once on the cheek and lips. He closed his eyes for one slow second, as he always did when she kissed him, before going to wash the traces of dough and flour from his hands.

And that would have been the last of it, except for the hysteria of me and my sister, our rehearsed re-enactments of our father's anger, his favourite sayings, and any comment even remotely related to sex. We squealed over each remark as a prize, smothering our shrieks into the sheets or yelling them out our shared window to be puzzled over by the late-night customers.

"No, thank you, Beena," said my sister. Her features were arch as she shrugged. "I don't get periods anymore."

"What?"

"From the running," she explained. "You know, like athletes."

Sadhana had started running in the mornings, taking herself on a daily forty-minute tour of the neighbourhood, a blur of coffee skin and black ponytail across rows of brownstone walkups, their owners just emerging, bending for their copy of *The Gazette* or *Le Journal* or locking their doors behind them as they descended with their black Labs or creamy Pomeranians, the dogs as twitchy and eager as Sadhana to get going. The pigeons that haunted our sidewalk fled before the speed of her runners, even though the birds were normally so tame my shoes would be almost clipping their tail feathers before they would rouse themselves to hop out of the way.

"Oh," I said. I stared at my sister and closed the medicine cabinet. "How extraordinary!"

"Isn't it?" she said. She winked, in her sudden, wicked way, and I thought she must be kidding.

"Yes, it is," I said. Then I chased her from the bathroom by sticking the tampon, still wrapped, in her ear, and slapping her on the bum until she shrieked and Uncle shouted for us both to be quiet.

UNCLE HAD MOVED INTO THE APARTMENT with the confidence of a deposed ruler returning to his kingdom, although until he came to Mile End to take over the bagel shop and the policing of our virtue he had never set foot in our small building, preferring to spend all his time in Dollard-Des-Ormeaux where he had a semi-detached house and a job as an accountant.

When he arrived he told us that our mother had

never liked him but that he wasn't going to hold it against us because he believed in doing his duty. We never told him that Mama used to call him an old crumbly who was still angry his brother married a white woman, even though Papa was twice the Sikh that he was.

"Your uncle thinks he's a believer, but his mind is too much on his money." Mama was never concerned so much with what people did, but more with what was in their hearts. Once when she put us to bed, her fingers lingered cool on my forehead as she said, "I wish I could know what you believed. Your sister's spirit is so open."

Where Papa had tiptoed as we slept, Uncle stomped in steel toes. Where Papa had deferred to our rightful ownership of the bathroom medicine cabinet, storing his modest toiletries in a neat zippered bag under the sink, Uncle scattered his combs and creams and bottlebrush of a toothbrush in a noxious formation around the sink. There they dripped and oozed and propagated further horrors, repelling us with as much force as if they were a voodoo ring of black magic.

THE FIRST CHANGE UNCLE MADE was to install himself at the front counter of the shop, in order to make what he called a personal connection with the clientele. He always called them the clientele, instead of the customers, or the folks, as Papa would have said. Uncle thought Papa had been a fool for keeping himself hidden away in the back, making bagels and keeping track of the books.

"What people want in this day and age is a little human connection," Uncle said. To which Sadhana said, "Yeah, that's why everywhere you go has ATMs," and he asked her what her poor dead Papa would say about her being impertinent to his only brother, which Sadhana must have taken as a rhetorical question because she didn't answer.

It was a testament to the bagels that the shop didn't go under. What Papa had said when he was alive was that Montrealers don't want their bagels served to them by a big, bearded Indian wearing a turban. He said he might be wrong about that, but didn't want to put it to the test. So it was interesting to see just how right he was, how the startled blink became another regular feature of the bagel exchange, as normal as the scanning of the chalkboard price list or the reaching for the tongs or the handing over of the money and the handing back of the change. Uncle either didn't see it or had decided he didn't care, alienating his clientele with boisterous small talk and broken French, exchanging awkward niceties until the line-up, which admittedly never dwindled, began to extend outside the door and down the front steps. I heard a woman saying she was always afraid that one day she was going to find a long beard-hair baked into her pumpernickel bagel.

"All I'm saying is I don't understand the point of making them wear hairnets if they're all going to have beards as long as Rip van Winkle." She had peered past Uncle into the open kitchen, where she could see Taran, with his trim goatee like a fine pencil embellishment, and Little Carlos, with his long, curling sideburns.

TARAN WAS RAVI'S COUSIN, and he was the one who got Ravi the job at the shop. Papa was always looking for workers because the store was open all night and there were always people quitting, people who became husbands or students or too weary to stay up late working next to the roaring fire of the wood oven and serving drunks into the early hours of the morning.

Papa hadn't trusted Ravi from the start. He came home and told us he might have hired a good-for-nothing but that he was going to wait and see before he fired him. Papa prided himself on his native intuition, and the satisfaction he took in being proven right was well worth the cost of a couple of burned batches of bagels or a few weeks' cash being skimmed off the top of the register. He was convinced that Ravi was a bad

Sikh and didn't trust his smooth-faced beauty or thick, expressive eyebrows.

"But you don't even know if his parents are *Khalsa*," I said. Keeping *Khalsa* meant staying pure according to Sikh law. In fact, it might have been the beauty of this word alone that caught my mother's interest, that spun the first strand in the web of her quest to become ever more blessed and complete, that led her to Canada, to yoga, to mantras, to gurus, to Sikhism and Papa.

"I don't need to know," he said. Papa had been interrogated by enough strangers about his religion that he'd developed a gentleman's code of never asking after anybody's origin or faith. "He looks guilty and that is enough."

Ravi might have looked guilty because by then he had already felt the shape of my breasts through the coarse wool of my sweater and had already run his hands along the small of my back under the cotton of my purple T-shirt. He had pursued me during his smoke breaks from the back door of the kitchen, which opened just below our small side balcony.

Our balcony faced into the alley, overlooking the big dumpsters where street kids and anarchists came scrounging for day-old bagels. The apartment's larger, main balcony faced into a courtyard, where other families had patio sets and barbeques and large planters overflowing with flowers. Papa wouldn't put any furniture out after the big controversy over having chairs in the temples, when he gave away every chair we owned to show support for the ban, but he whitewashed the concrete and kept it swept and bought a large, colourful woven mat.

"Why you two always sit out on that little ledge of a balcony, I will never understand." He said this every time he saw me and Sadhana dragging the old burgundy floor cushions toward the sliding doors.

"Because it's us-sized, Papa," Sadhana said.

But once the door slid shut behind us, we stretched out to wait for the boys to appear, dragging the garbage to the bins, lighting cigarettes or hauling in logs when the truck came with firewood for the ovens. Clad in white aprons, their skin streaked with soot and smelling, we guessed, like fire and sweat, these boys seemed to emerge from another world, riotous in their jokes, swearing and hooting and pretending to fight.

I was in love with their muscled limbs, even risking being seen in order to catch a glimpse of their strong forearms, so veined and dark with hair. Sadhana liked to listen to their voices, burying her face in the cushion and whispering their names to me as she learned each of their voices in turn, repeating their phrases as they spoke, murmuring words to me in French, English, Punjabi.

At first, Sadhana was my conspirator, calling out Ravi's name when we spotted him alone, prodding me toward the edge of the balcony to start a conversation. But once it really started, once I was sneaking downstairs at night to see him, something changed, making it hard to think about him in the daytime.

Ravi was older, though he hadn't started university. He said he wanted to go into business administration, because he claimed he could talk anybody into anything, but it seemed to me that he was a little too fumbling, too ingratiating, to be able to manage employees. Sadhana pressed for more details about him and sulked when I offered nothing more than a story he had told me about catching his brother masturbating in the bathroom. It was the only time he had ever made me laugh.

I couldn't find the words to explain that the thing with Ravi was like an exercise, an obstacle course. Like the Canada Fitness Test that we used to do in school. The gaudy participation badges were still pinned up around the edges of our bulletin board, the embroidery thread like wound filaments lashing us to the girls we used to be. Sadhana, gold, stubborn and bright. Me, silver, clingy and hesitant. Vague.

It was how I remembered feeling as a child, when
Sadhana and I raced to the corner and every once in a
while I would suddenly pull ahead, the energy rushing
outward from the centre of my body, my cheeks flushing
with warmth and elation. The sound of my feet and the
noises of the street would recede and all I could hear was
myself thinking *this is really happening* as loud as though I'd
spoken it. It was like that with Ravi, every time we were
alone. Only it was like he was the race, or maybe even the
pavement.

"I was just seeing how far I could go," I said. "To see
what we could do."

"I don't believe that," said Sadhana, and I knew she
was hurt because she wanted to counsel me, and because
she thought I was trying to keep to myself my newfound
knowledge of boys and their bodies: their ravenous ap-
petites, their strange, fleshy mounds. But I couldn't see
why she would be surprised by what I was doing, given
all our eavesdropping and secret plans, all the fantasies
we described and even wrote down and whispered to
each other across the darkness of our bedroom. It could
only be that she wanted to be first, like always.

"I'm not in love with him," I said. "I don't think I
could love any of the bagel boys."

I didn't mean this, or have any reason to mean this,

besides a need to offer some kind of explanation of why Ravi, who was so beautiful, didn't move me. It knew it was the kind of capricious decree that Sadhana would admire. I covered my eyes with my fingers, cupped my cheeks, shook my head as she frowned at me and twisted her wristful of silver bangles. Finally I shrugged. "I liked the feeling of putting myself into their world."

"It's slutty to have sex without love," she said, with an unusual tremor of judgment, and I wondered how she could really feel that way. After everything we had heard the bagel boys talk about, why should it be any different for us?

IT WAS RAVI WHO TOLD PAPA about our situation, twisting up his apron as he looked at the floor, promising to marry me right after my graduation.

"She's just a month gone," he said. "She won't even be showing. Beena's a big enough girl that nobody would even have to know."

Papa's eyes bulged and he slammed the metal counter with his fist.

"You think I came here so my daughter gets married like this?" Papa pulled at his shirt collar with his left hand, grabbing Ravi's shoulder with his right. He shook him, hard, as the bagel boys whooped and catcalled.

Little Carlos told me afterward that he was so interested in seeing what was going on that he burned himself flipping the next batch out of the oven, and in all the uproar nobody noticed his thunderous cursing.

"This shame cannot be hidden," said Papa. "Someone will have to pay for this dishonour!"

Ravi pulled away and ran out the back door, faster than I could shout his name from the balcony where I waited beneath a quilt, my stomach a sick knot under my mother's favourite sweater. My father turned and clutched his left arm and said my name but died before he could tell me I had ruined things, which was the only part of the whole nightmare that was worth being glad about, or so Sadhana said later. Ravi came to the funeral where Sadhana stole glances at me as she mocked his hair, his clothes, his face.

"I heard that Ravi was short for ravishing," she said in a stage whisper, "but I find that a little hard to believe. I guess he's just short for no apparent reason."

A couple of the bagel boys snorted, and Ravi gave me a nervous look as Sadhana nudged me, her elbow a prod in my side for appreciation. I shook my head, and she glared. Then Sadhana spit in Ravi's face. She called him a coward, and he fled. She thought the fight was only about Papa finding out that I had a boyfriend.

"Thanks for ruining our lives with your puppy love,"

she had said as we were dressing, which rankled because she was almost two years younger than I was. And because I knew from that moment, as I watched her apply two coats of waterproof mascara and then straighten the skirt of her black dress, unworn since Mama's funeral the year before, that she blamed me for everything.

LITTLE CARLOS BECAME MY CONFIDANT as Sadhana pulled away and Ravi became a pale memory of smoky breath and clutching fingers, vague compared to our shame, already making itself prominent through my almost constant nausea. I longed now to hear more from Sadhana about Ravi's foolishness, his cowardice, his unworthiness, but she and I only seemed to talk from opposite sides of the bathroom door. Mostly, I just banged for entry and asked what on earth could be taking so long. By now she knew I was pregnant, though it was still a secret from Uncle, the bagel boys exhibiting uncommon discretion under Little Carlos's direction. She always emerged from the bathroom with her teeth freshly brushed, her black hair smoothed and flipped back.

"All yours, big sis," she'd say as I pushed past her. "Heave ho."

I thought maybe she was pulling out her hair, because it seemed, as I knelt over the toilet, waiting for the lurching in my stomach to subside, that there was more black hair on the floor than normal, more than the usual two or three wigs' worth yielded over the course of a regular bathroom cleaning. My own hair was becoming thick as a broom as my shame grew larger, and I braided it and kept it pinned up until the point in every afternoon at which my head began to ache from the weight.

Sadhana and I never cut our hair, keeping our heads hirsute and Samson-strong and just the way any old-fashioned deity intended. With our coarse black body hair, though, my sister and I had decided to take liberties with the pronouncements of the holy Gurus. We collected razors, hoarded bottles of Nair, melted strips of wax in the microwave. Shaving in our house was so taboo that we didn't dare mention it even to our mother. Mama was flexible on many points of religious doctrine, but she'd given up shaving in the sixties.

"We're beautiful the way we are, kittens," she said, and that was that.

Sadhana didn't believe that our mother, a natural redhead, would ever be sympathetic to our burgeoning moustaches.

"If it was freckles we were worried about," she used to say, "she might take us more seriously."

—

"DO YOU WANT TO COOK SOMETHING TERRIBLE for Uncle?" I asked Sadhana. Sometimes we made supper and stirred extra spoonfuls of salt or curry powder into Uncle's bowl, then watched as the sweat sprang up over his face, moistening the hair of his beard and moustache. Sadhana said he would be reincarnated as a raccoon, because he was a rotten human being who would eat anything. We had watched raccoons sniffing around the bagel dumpsters, scrabbling with their clever little hands. They got trapped inside, sometimes, if the bins weren't secured, and had to be helped out with a long wooden plank set at an angle, kept by Papa for just such occasions.

In the weeks after Papa died, Uncle held his tongue, choking down half of whatever we set before him, but after two months of such suppers, he lost his temper and shouted at us, spit clinging to the corners of his thick, chapped lips. The eruption came when Sadhana offered to pour him more water and he said that what he would prefer instead would be a time machine to take us back to when our goddamn hippie mother could teach us to cook properly, if in fact she'd ever known how herself.

"I'd like that, too," said Sadhana. "I would like nothing better, in fact." And she stalked off to our bedroom without looking back, as Uncle, muttering, emptied his bowl into the garbage.

Now, again, she was avoiding me, gazing instead at a magazine, scratching her left calf with the toenails of her right foot. Projecting a poised economy of movement and emotion.

"That's kids' stuff," she said. "Those cooking pranks." Her face was placid. "I'm over it." She flipped the page and her shoulder inched up in a minute shrug of dismissal.

I wondered if she was only talking about the pranks, or if she was saying that she'd broken away from the sting of Uncle's awfulness, the misery channelled into all the ruined meals. Either way I had a feeling she was lying.

I ASKED LITTLE CARLOS WHETHER HE'D NOTICED a change in Sadhana. He was sitting on the cement stoop outside the shop's back door, his black Doc Martens greyed by the same sprinkling of flour that I once cleaned from my father's Oxfords. It was like a dusting of baby powder, only to me sweeter, redolent of a simpler and happier past.

"Do you think she's trying to thin her hair?" I thought of the alien lightness of blonde hair, the fine wispiness of a yellow ponytail, and the futile envy that sometimes seized me and my sister and made us want to shed our skins, sloughing off our difference like so much dead tissue.

Little Carlos shook his head and kicked at some ash on the ground. "No. Are you crazy?" He looked up. "She's shrunk to a whittled toothpick."

"What?"

"A year ago you two were almost the same size. Now you can hide a baby in your belly with no one noticing and Sadhana is about as big as Véronique." Véronique was Little Carlos's infant daughter.

"She's just running a lot," I said, frowning. "Every day. That's bound to make anyone pretty skinny." I pushed back my shoulders against the cold brick of the shop's outside wall, resisting the constant slump that tended to push out my stomach.

He shrugged as he stood up. "Maybe so, Beena. But she looks starving to me."

I LOOKED WHEN I WAS LYING IN BED, in the golden light of my reading lamp. With her back turned to me, asleep facing the wall, Sadhana was finally still enough for me to really see her, to be able to make out the shape of her vertebrae through her yellow nightshirt, a string of giant beads down her back. I realized that when I thought about my sister, fixing her in my mind, I was seeing a different version of her, an outdated version. It was like when I thought about Mama, picturing her as I remembered her from my earliest memories, wearing dashikis in a multitude of colours, a different one for every day of the week, over tight brown leggings. But sometimes I looked at photos taken the year she died, and I saw her grey streaks, her calmer smile, the laugh lines like riverbeds.

"You're sick," I said aloud, but Sadhana didn't stir.

In the morning, once I heard the stomp of Uncle's boots leaving, I got up and made oatmeal, stirring in twice Mama's recommended amount of brown sugar. I put in cinnamon because Sadhana liked it. She came to the table wearing Mama's brown chenille robe and pink terry cloth slippers, clutching the wooden candy bowl from the living room.

She watched me eating. Her lips were pursed like when she used to watch grown-ups kissing, or when Mama scooped the tub drain free of hair. She unwrapped a Werther's original, flattening the wrapper between her thumbs in a practised gesture as the toffee-flavoured candy travelled inside her mouth from cheek to cheek.

"It makes me sick just looking at that," she said. She nodded to the bowl of porridge I'd placed before her.

"Really?" I said. "I thought you made yourself sick by sticking your finger down your throat."

Sadhana stared, then sobbed, then threw her bowl of oatmeal at me.

ONCE I HAD FOUND OUT HER SECRET, Sadhana became less obvious about her habits. I still swept up all her falling-out hair, watching it weave itself into dust nets on the end of the broom, but she no longer closed herself in the bathroom after every meal. Instead, she threw up when I was out or asleep, and she ate like a sick bird, living off mint tea and hard candies.

Some of the guys from the shop started calling her Nervosa behind her back. Carlos, who had pleaded for the removal of his prefix on the grounds that Big Carlos had quit over three years ago, tried to stamp it out, but Sadhana had already begun shedding her friends like her pounds, responding to the joking advances of the bagel boys with scornful remarks drained of her once-playful wit.

It seemed that sarcasm had dripped away from her along with the weight of her hips and the roundness of her cheeks and shoulders. I wondered if it was possible for her irony to have been buried in her thighs, or for her sense of humour to have squatted in the dimples of flesh on her arms or in some other part of her that used to exist but had since melted away, merging into the dust and moisture of the air, or into the dankness of the river that led away from our bathroom pipes.

"SHE'LL COME AROUND," SAID CARLOS. Sadhana was asleep and I was outside by the back door of the shop, whispering with Carlos on his break.

"There's a baby on the way," he said. "That'll snap her out of it."

Everyone knew about the baby now, even Uncle, who had officially washed his hands of us and spent all his time in the shop or at the coffee house down the street. The coffee house was favoured by men much older than he was, yet even they provided no match for his bitterness and deep suspicion about the younger generation.

"Maybe," I said. I watched Carlos's face, trying to make out the emotion in his dark blue eyes. The smaller and more breakable Sadhana became, the more Carlos seemed to take an interest in her. Trying to visualize my legs as tree trunks planted in the earth, I asked him if there wasn't something more about Sadhana that made him so concerned.

"Uncle never mentions it," I said. "Maybe it isn't as serious as we think."

Carlos snorted. "Why use your uncle as an example

for anything? We both know he knows nothing." He paused. "But you're right." He blinked, the lighter tips of his long eyelashes glimmering in the glow of the streetlamp. "There's a beauty in seeing the parts that make something up. Like looking at a finished puzzle up close, or the inside of an old alarm clock."

He meant the glimpses of Sadhana's new skinny body, the bones so plainly visible beneath her skin. The ribcage like the frame of a wooden schooner, only partially built. The shoulder blades like axe-heads ready to slice through skin.

I glared. "You really do like girls to be as skinny as models." Julie, his daughter's mother, was a chain-smoking size zero who sometimes came to the shop to pick up her child-support cheques.

"No," said Carlos. He put his hands on my waist and slid them down over my hips. "I like girls like you."

I WAS GETTING LARGER EVERY DAY, EXPANDING, and, in a way, feeling more expansive every day, too. I tried baking bread—a superfluous act of magnanimity for someone living over a bagel shop—and when, through neglect, it failed to rise, I threw it to the birds with the same cheerful unconcern I felt for my wasted attempts at peanut butter cookies, chocolate cake, and lemon meringue pie.

Instead I bought dainties at the store, hoping to provide an appetite-inducing accompaniment to the counselling sessions Sadhana had started the day after we cried over the oatmeal.

But Sadhana continued to lose weight and seemed to be turning inward, saving what was left of herself for herself. She lay on the couch when she came home from school and frowned as I crumbled the darkened crust of bread between my palms and scattered it to the birds on the balcony. Carlos had bought me a lawn chair so that I could sit outside in the late autumn heat in relative comfort. I left the patio door open to make sure I could hear anything Sadhana happened to volunteer.

"We're just going to end up with more pigeon shit out there," she said. She looked even more disagreeable than she sounded. The fat had dropped off her face and left her with more frown lines on her forehead, the extra skin folding itself into deep horizontal furrows.

"Don't worry," I said, but the pigeons were already flustering the sparrows pecking at the ragged crumbs at my feet. I flexed each swollen foot in turn to ensure the safety of my toes, and four sparrows fled to the railing, frightened by the creak of the lawn chair as I shifted my weight. The pigeons seized upon the bread, clicking across the concrete with their terrible red feet.

"Their toes are so loud," complained Sadhana, and I made a show of shushing the pigeons, my index finger upright at my lips. She gave a laugh like a throaty cough.

"I'm sorry," she said. "I'm horrible. I'm a disaster."

"No."

"Yes." She propped herself up on elbows so sharp they creased the couch. "Where is Mama when we finally need her advice?" The bleating worry in her voice made me push myself up and go to her. I touched one puffy hand to her hollow face and found that I had nothing to say.

MAMA LIKED TO MAKE EMOTIONAL ANALOGIES. She confessed that at one time, before Papa, she used to smoke hashish out of a glass pipe with her girlfriends and lie around on an orange cushion composing poetry.

She told us that love was fragrant and inviting like a bowl of warm, pink water from which rose petals have only just been removed. And also like the thick juice surrounding canned peach slices or halves. Sweet and sticky. Or like *amrit*, the nectar of sugar water that a Sikh drinks at initiation.

One day, before either of us had started high school, a fly drowned in some fruit salad I'd left out on the table and became Mama's inspiration for that day's sermon of inspired platitudes.

"Love is a trap, my pets," Mama said.

Her tiny cherub's face telegraphed enthusiasm as the apples of her cheeks bobbed up and down in delight. She was spreading honey on toast, and the earnest level of her eyebrows, raised almost to her hairline, seemed to emphasize the goodness that tended to transform all of her commonplace wisdom into sage advice. "The most delicious trap you could ever hope to get stuck in."

"But the fly's dead now, Mama," said Sadhana.

"Well, that's what love is about, too, my darling." Mama's eyes sparkled, two glistening teacups, bone-china circles against the porcelain platter of her face. "Pain and separation and death. The death of the self." She twisted a lock of Sadhana's black hair between her fingers. "You aren't ready for love if you aren't ready for pain."

Sadhana rolled her eyes. Her fingers drummed the table.

"Mama," she said. "Are you trying to scare us?"

But Mama shook her head. "Coming together with another human being is a process that hurts just as much being torn apart. It's just another kind of reorganization, a kind of creation that can be as dynamic as dissolution." Mama leaned back, as she always did when she flexed her vocabulary, and rubbed her arms with her hands.

"Wait and see, my loves," she said between bites of toast, licking the honey from where it caught at the corner of her lips. "When he cries, you cry. When he bleeds, you bleed."

"Oh, Mama," I said. "You're so dramatic."

Sadhana looked puzzled. "When does Papa cry?" she asked.

THE DAY AFTER CARLOS STROKED MY BELLY and said "Hello, little one," Sadhana tripped on the stairs and broke her wrist. Her bones had turned brittle, and I imagined them hollowed out, changed into rolled tubes of parchment where we had written all of our secrets and repressed despair.

I felt guilty, as though I had helped to empty her out by failing to give her anything to compensate for everything that had been taken away. After Mama died, Sadhana used to ask me whether I wasn't sad and wrap her arm around my shoulders as her tears fell on my neck and hair.

"I miss her so much all the time," she would say. "And I feel so bad for Papa."

And I would murmur something in agreement and lean my head down against hers, letting it rest there until her sniffling came to a stop and our breathing fell into a rhythm. But when I tried to think about how I was feeling, it was like searching for keys dropped outside in winter: the numbing cold of a hand moving through snow, the sharpness of wet metal on flesh, and my fingers fumbling, shaking, dropping the keys again as I tried to fit them into the lock. It was as though I couldn't bring myself to the trouble of trying to get in, because I dreaded what lay before me. But now I saw that Sadhana had already been inside. Waiting.

I WEPT NOW AS SHE LAY in the living room while I tried to cook all her favourite foods, looking through a battered copy of *The Joy of Cooking* and the red metal box with Mama's handwritten recipe cards. My belly kept me so far back from the stove that my arms grew tired from the stirring. The curry stung my nose and lent me an excuse for my leaky face.

"Doesn't this smell good?" I asked. I blinked as I turned back to look at her. The narrow white cast on her arm gave it the look of bare bone. I had signed it "I love you" with a black marker. And Carlos wrote, "Eat."

"Yes," said Sadhana. She shifted slightly. "Maybe I'll be reincarnated in your baby," she said, and I trembled. Sadhana talked a lot about the baby, but I could only think about the birth: all the pain and the blood that was coming for me.

I spooned out a little bowl for her into one of our old Holly Hobbie dishes, Holly's face forever hidden by her huge blue bonnet. I remembered how Sadhana used to covet her ruffled patchwork pinafore, while I envied Holly the privacy of her big hat. It was strange to think of Mama choosing such quaint and precious dishes, and even stranger to think that we would keep on changing, while she, who showed us how to change, would stay the same forever.

Attempting a smile, I said, "I doubt it."

Sadhana gave a soft laugh. "Are you saying you aren't a believer?"

"No," I said. The curry was so hot it burned my fingers through the old melamine as I carried it to her. "Just the opposite."

Scar Tissue

PATTI THINKS THERE IS TOO MUCH to be packed up and put away. She sits at the kitchen table, tapping a spatula against a saucepan, breathing in the musty rich fragrance of saffron rice undercut with cardboard. The boxes surrounding her are half-filled, jumbled with possessions she can no longer account for: a large wooden spool with four nails in the end, a feathered headband shedding yellow fluff, an aged maraca made from a gourd. The beginning of packing is always like this, with Patti moving from room to room, picking up things that seem strange and dropping them into the first boxes of nonessentials, things she won't need again until she gets to wherever it is she is going to be.

If David were home, he would urge her to throw this stuff out, call her a pack rat, toss her a black garbage bag from under the counter. Patti prefers to save decisions about what's worth keeping until later, after she's settled. But the muddled boxes have a look of commotion about them, like the beginning of a desperate journey, and Patti gets up to move them one by one out of sight beneath the blue-checked cover of the kitchen table.

The boxes squeak as she slides them along the linoleum, and the babies in their playpen, on the other side of the plastic gate, respond with quiet blather. Clara, three, who can climb in and out of the playpen at will, leans against its mesh side, peering at a picture book in her lap, muttering as she turns its thick board pages. Benjamin, who is almost old enough to crawl, lies on his stomach at her feet, regarding a stuffed rabbit and cooing at it as though expecting a response. Outside, through the opened patio door, Ryan tosses a ball in the back yard. His blue eyes are narrowed in a squint as he fumbles every catch with a glove still too big for his hand.

Patti watches the steam escaping from the pot of rice, then turns back to the table. She has the paraphernalia of moving lined up before her like instruments in an operating theatre. Unmade boxes, scissors, packing tape, two black Sharpie markers in case one gets mislaid. Moving is a procedure. Pen and paper for the detailed master list that she will type up and print before they pack the computer. Once she gets somewhere new, Patti likes being able to find things right away. Light bulbs. A frying pan. Her black leather skirt. Now that she has children this is even more important. Thermometers, teething rings, favourite toys. The children, like her, are needy, fussy, and fragile. Patti believes in humouring them.

When a bee flies in the opened patio door with a drone like a passing motorbike, Patti gives an involuntary shriek. Ryan runs inside as Benjamin starts to wail, his cries beginning with a slow sputter before he commits himself to unhappiness.

What's the matter? asks Ryan, taking Patti by the wrist. Ryan has a strange solicitousness when it comes to Patti. David thinks this is because Ryan carries an unconscious memory of abandonment, from when his real mother dropped him off at the age of two with only a pair of red pyjamas and a knapsack full of ID. Patti thinks Ryan just likes to model himself after his father.

Nothing's the matter, sweetheart, she says. I was startled by a bee that snuck up on me.

Tiptoe, says Clara from the playpen. One red curl tucked in the corner of her mouth escapes and shines with spit. Patti is always surprised by the eclecticism of childhood vocabulary. The planets, anvils, and double-barrelled dinosaurs that make appearances before words like picnic or daydream. Shhhhhhh, Clara says, either to the bee or to her brother.

The bee flies out, but Benjamin is still upset, and Patti steps over the plastic gate and bends to lift him to her chest. Ryan begins to follow, but the gate is high and sturdy even for a seven-year-old, and he knows better than to try to shift it without asking. Since Clara's accident, Patti doesn't let the littlest ones in the kitchen.

The phone rings. Grasping Ben in a firm hold, Patti reaches to answer the cordless, propped on its wall charger beside her.

Is David there? A woman's voice she doesn't recognize.

No, I'm afraid not. Would you like to leave a message?

But the phone has already gone dead.

David, not Mr. McAdams, or David McAdams even.

PATTI MET DAVID AT A POETRY READING where she was playing flute to accompany Grizzald, a spoken word artist she'd met in a high school jazz band.

Grizzald used to be called Graham, said Patti, revolving her beer bottle on the aged wooden table. He wore plaid pants and played the drums.

Condensation ran over her fingers. Looking at David sitting across from her, where he'd planted himself after asking for tips on getting into the poetic flautist business, she realized why she'd agreed to do something so exhibitionist. She took in his fitted olive T-shirt and wondered if anyone was watching them.

I ran into Grizzald at the grocery store a couple weeks back, Patti said. The veggie burger section. He asked whether I'd be up for a gig. I hadn't played in ages, of course, but I still had my flute and thought I could fake it well enough for a bunch of literary types. She raised an eyebrow, implicating herself in the slight. Lit student, she said, thumb at her chest. Patti.

David clinked his beer bottle to hers. Cheers, he said, holding her gaze. You know, it's seven years of bad sex if you don't look someone in the eye when you toast them.

Cheers, said Patti. I didn't know that. I may already be doomed.

When David told her his name, Patti blinked. She had just read one of his articles in the Saturday paper, an interdisciplinary essay tying together photography, literature, and popular culture. It turned out he was a prolific freelancer.

You're what they call a man of letters.

Why, I suppose so, said David. He looked pleased and downed a third of his beer.

Patti said she was impressed that he made enough to live on, and David admitted that he also taught at colleges.

In fact, I principally teach at colleges, he said. She laughed.

He bought her another beer and they talked about books.

When Patti decided to take a ride home with Grizzald, David gave her his card. She rubbed her thumb over the black embossed letters before putting it in the back pocket of her jeans.

I don't have a card, said Patti. But I work mornings at the Wheat Stone. I'm the pastry chef.

Patti cake, David said.

THE HOUSE THEY'RE MOVING TO is two neighbourhoods over from where they've been living, a place where the yards are bigger and where semi-detached townhouses like the one they're in now are a rarity. The new house has five bedrooms, a sprouting vegetable garden, and a wide front veranda that makes

Patti think of porch swings and Technicolor movies about the Old South.

David had wanted to use the settlement money to get a house with a pool, but Patti worried it would be tempting fate. She happens to know that backyard swimming pool drownings are the second-leading cause of accidental death in toddlers, after car accidents. She has memorized a number of these facts, as though with a catalogue of statistics she might buffet away risk, like a hitter batting out fastballs from the plate.

She is already nervous about the unknown hazards that await them. At their current home, she has kept a mental archive, a register for her vigilance: the long, worn rug in the hallway with a tendency to slip away underfoot; the basement door that flies open, yawning black and grim down the steep pitch of its staircase. The front window that bangs down on sluggish fingers. The gas stove. At the new place, it will be all surprise, something Patti rarely finds cause to welcome.

DAVID SAYS THEY OWE THE NEW HOUSE to his friend Paul. Paul is a lawyer, a litigator. The one who knew to go after the nightgown manufacturer.

The nightgown was an acrylic velour, in deep purple with a flowing pink trim. Jan, David's mother, picked it up at a garage sale. She had a good eye for treasure and a great memory for the holes in Patti's household stock.

I noticed you don't have a cast-iron skillet, she said, carrying over a green enamelled pan, the wooden handle only slightly scorched. It's Le Creuset, she said. It'll last forever. She had a reverence that Patti didn't quite understand.

Thanks, said Patti.

Later, Jan brought over a toy Patti had mentioned from her own childhood, a telephone on red wheels with lolling eyes and a tuneful locomotion.

Fisher-Price classic, said Jan. Now it's like you've passed it down to Clara and Ben.

Then there were the things Patti hadn't realized she wanted until she saw them: a crystal punch bowl with twenty shallow glasses hanging along its scalloped rim. Favourite board games for the kids, like Clue and Monopoly, their pieces and cards carefully enumerated by Jan for completeness.

The nightgown was a little big, but Clara adored it. Dwess, she called it. She cried every time Patti peeled it off her to get it in the wash.

IT WENT UP IN A FLASH, melting right into the skin. It was David who told his mother how it happened, though it would have come out later, anyway, with the lawsuit. Jan was devastated.

I guess there are regulations now, she said to Patti, her voice catching, with the manufacturing and all. New safety stuff for kids' clothes. I never thought.

Me neither, said Patti.

PAUL THE LITIGATOR SAID, it's a good thing you've done here, but Patti couldn't be so sure. A struggling Canadian textile company settled out of court and went under. And now Patti and David were about to move out of their small but perfectly serviceable house into a three-storey home. Hadn't she read somewhere that on average Canadians had the largest houses in the world? She thinks it may only give them more space in which to be apart from one another.

PATTI FIRST MET RYAN a few weeks after she and David were married. Blossom, his mother, appeared outside their walkup apartment in a beige Toyota Tercel with a faulty muffler. She was young and exceptionally beautiful. She was carrying Ryan, who was two, still asleep against her chest even after the noise of the drive and his removal from the car.

I thought you might want to finally meet your son,

she said, when David and Patti answered the door.

Okay, said David.

Blossom was wearing a jean skirt made from cutoffs and a low, tight yellow tank top. There was studied impatience in the way she clattered her silver bangles up and down her arms, swinging her dark hair back behind her shoulders. She had a sensuous, no-nonsense air about her, as though anything not sensuous might strike her as nonsense. For Ryan, she had a gentle but not inefficient touch. With the fluidity of one motion, she wiped his mouth, stroked his cheek with her thumb, pushed his hair out of his face and patted him once on the head as she passed him off to David.

Aren't you going to invite me in? she said, swabbing the back of her arm against the spot of drool Ryan had left at the top of her breast.

Inside, Blossom ignored Patti, who poured herself a glass of iced tea and went to sit on the balcony. She thought about Blossom's name and remembered a guy she had dated in university, so repressed and fresh out of Bible college that he could scarcely walk by flowers without blushing. They just seem obscene, he'd said, when Patti mentioned it. All those sex organs blooming in plain sight.

It wasn't long before she heard the door slam. When she heard a rumbling sound on the street, she came back inside, setting her glass down in the sink with a measure of resolve. She strode into the living room to find Ryan stirring on David's lap.

She said she would be right back, said David. His voice sounded strained. He said, she told me she had some photos in the car.

DAVID HAD CONTACTED PAUL, who tried and failed to track Blossom down. In Ryan's tiny backpack she had left only his immunization records, a half-emptied bottle of orange Triaminic, and his birth certificate, with David listed as the father.

Paul said, what a cold-hearted bitch.

David said only, I think she was pissed I got married. His face was mild.

Ryan himself was sweet and seemed only slightly bereft. Patti tried to figure out what to do and ended up taking a leave from work.

I didn't think he was ever going to be a part of our lives, David told her by way of apology. Blossom left town and never got in touch with me again. It hurt to even imagine him.

Patti watched his face and believed him. He described Blossom as a two-night stand he'd met just before Patti, though Patti figured they had probably dated.

It might have been their ages, as David had almost

twelve years on Patti, or his natural reticence when it came to talking about himself, or some basic, preserving part of her that didn't want to ask, but they had never done a big rundown of previous lovers. Over the few years they'd been together, Patti had, more or less, told him about everybody in one way or another, but David's litany had long gaps. When Patti told herself the story of his life, there were more lacunae than points of substance to make it up from.

This is the way to do it, said David one day, his hand on her waist as they watched Ryan in the park. Get our babies by delivery. No morning sickness, no swollen ankles. No wretched mood swings and absurd fights.

Patti wondered if he had seen Blossom during her pregnancy. She said only, well, there are some things about making babies that do interest me.

RYAN LOOKS EXACTLY LIKE DAVID, as though his mother was only an incubator, a transcriptionist, rather than the author of half his genes. The same white-blonde hair, the same blue eyes like glacial runoff, clear and almost aquamarine. A slight cleft to the chin and already a hint of David's cheekbones, the kind that Patti would have paid money for if she believed in that sort of thing.

David's looks are the flint in their fire. She had always

dated intelligent men, the bookish, self-deprecating kind who let her in on every joke. But David is a different kind of animal, a writer and scholar in the body of a farmer, strong and broad enough to be hooked up to a yoke himself. Patti responds to him with a bare appetite that leaves no room for her usual embarrassment.

Once the kids are asleep, he kicks aside two boxes of her winter sweaters, steering her by her hips toward the bed.

You should pack up all of your clothes, he says, laying her down. Every last little thing.

He stares her in the eyes as they touch each other, noses her face in what feels like affection. She wants to shrink from the intensity of his gaze. At the same time, she likes the heavy, sumptuous feeling of being seen by him.

You have the most beautiful eyes, says David, cupping her face in his hands. I could lose myself.

But it is in these moments that Patti herself feels found, as though a simpler version of her has been created, summoned out of skin and sweat. She can slip it on like a dressing gown, one as bright and redemptive as a life jacket.

Afterward, he brings her a warm, wet cloth, already wrung out.

A whole new bedroom soon, he says. Just think.

Patti says, I missed you all day today. The phone kept ringing and it wasn't you.

I'm here now, says David. Right now.

RYAN IS HERS, AND YET HE ISN'T. Like David. Like even Clara and Benjamin, if Patti is truly honest with herself, though she thinks this only at her gloomiest, most philosophical moments, usually when she is cleaning the bathroom or doing some other task she does not enjoy. She thinks, they will grow up and give themselves to other people, and those other people will be more important to them than I am. She broods about this as she puts away the groceries, stacking cans of tuna into a tower of her future supplanters: friends, girlfriends, boyfriends, wives, husbands. Children. Lovers.

Patti's initial approach to Ryan was one of loose affection, mindful of the day Blossom might choose to reappear. But no matter how breezy or unconditional she tries to feel, she lies awake fretting that he will be seized without warning.

David's attempts to comfort her are practical. I'm his father, he says. If she comes back, I'll still have rights. Then, with his thick fingers buried in the hair at the base of her skull, he kisses her forehead, rolling her over to face him. And you've got rights over me, he says. In case you'd forgotten. Then his hand, pulling hers to his chest and sliding it down.

In the daytime, Patti cannot believe her claims on David to be any less tenuous or circumstantial than her claims on his son. She feels as though she merely stepped within the frequency of romance and the world responded. At the wedding, David's friends and family seemed both congratulatory and amazed, and Patti sensed their confusion because she felt it herself. She tells herself, it was timing, that's all. He thought it was time to settle down. And then to test out how it feels, she thinks, no, it's me, I'm special. I'm the One.

JAN COMES OVER EVERY TUESDAY AND THURSDAY while David teaches at the university. She started coming by after the accident. The first dressing changes were at the hospital, where they had special beds and basins and drugs to help manage the pain as the doctors monitored for infection. David was the best at tending Clara's wounds, and after they realized this, he mostly took it over. But at first it was Patti and Jan, facing each other from either side of Clara's bed, scarcely able to find a place where their eyes could safely come to rest. The parts of Clara's body that hadn't burned in the fire had been harvested for skin that could be grafted. Her face remained intact, but her expression was so weary and enduring that Patti felt it as a reproach.

You show too much, David told Patti. She looks at you and knows to be upset.

When David bathed Clara, or rubbed cream on her dry, grafted skin to keep it moist, Clara only cried silently, holding back the plaintive whine that came out under Patti's touch.

My brave girl, he said. My precious girl.

While Patti divides the kids' clothing into boxes according to seasons, Jan begins packing the books. Between them, David and Patti have seven tall bookcases, all full, the shelves double-stacked and teeming. Jan moves from one bookcase to the next, sealing and labelling according to Patti's instructions.

She says, you've got some doubles here between the collections. Maybe it's time to pare down. Do you need two copies of *As I Lay Dying*?

I'd rather not, says Patti. Her hands smooth the wrinkles out of Ryan's woolen pants. Jan shrugs.

I guess you'll have room at the new place for more bookcases, says Jan. But these copies are identical. Same edition, same everything. She fits both books into the top of a box, closing the flap with her knee as she bends to tape it shut.

You just never know, Patti says, and Jan looks at her.

What don't you know? asks Jan. After a silence, she says, I suppose not.

They are interrupted by the phone ringing. When Patti returns, Jan smiles, eyes questioning.

David?

Patti shakes her head. Hang-up, she says.

Patti begins sorting the clothes at a faster clip, packing items in only an approximation of folding. When she finds two of David's shirts mixed in with Ryan's things, she tosses them to the centre of the room, away from her other piles. They balloon out then deflate on descent, tasteful olive-green and blue-slate puddles on the hardwood floor, plastic buttons clicking like landing gear as they make contact.

David should be home by now, she says. Her irritation is obvious, and a pucker stops up Jan's lips. Patti knows David is the magnet that pulled Jan east after a lifetime on the prairies. The favourite.

He's probably working late, says Jan. Her short, grey ponytail swings as she nods. He's a hard worker. You know, when Jack died, he took care of everything, even the farm for half a year.

I know. You're right.

He's a good man, says Jan.

Yes, says Patti.

SHE THINKS OF CLARA'S LARGE SCAR AS SEAWEED. It has that kind of shape, aquatic fronds, rounded fingers of raspberry skin clasping her daughter's arms and shoulders, a shrug of mottled pink and cream across the top of her back. Patti sometimes imagines it as a shadow cast by sunlight filtered through shallow, reedy water, kelp waving in gentle tides behind Clara, who is wading or maybe scuba-diving, turned away to face the ocean.

David has a scar, too. It cleaves his upper lip, a mean kind of rift on the right-hand side, a suggestion of latent strength and violence. The product of a bar brawl he stumbled into during his twenties on a trip around Britain. The scar tells a lie, Patti knows, for David is a peaceable man, not cruel, attentive to the force of his body. But in the end she suspects it is only half a lie, that in the two decades David has lived with it, the scar has wrought its own adjustments as he has grown into the man that it implies, accepting its quiet prospects and restrictions.

On one of their first dates, Patti traced the scar with her finger as they lay naked across his unmade bed. She shuddered to think of his mouth cut open, his beautiful face gaped and bleeding like a fish on a lure.

You like my scar, David said. He had his arms crossed behind his head, neck resting on his wrists.

Only the very sexiest women like my scar.

He was talking in the staccato twang he used for flirting, his prairie hick talk, eyes looking solemn, but something else, maybe the very curl in his lip where the scar tugged it upwards, making his words come out ironic.

Uh-huh, said Patti. I bet.

Patti has only one scar, on her wrist. One round pink dot the size of a pencil eraser, from a chicken pox pock she couldn't resist picking. Before Clara was born, David used to say he wondered how she managed to float through life so unscathed.

Don't know, she said. Lucky, I guess.

Later, but before the accident, he pointed to her stretch marks. He said, I did that. Or at least I helped.

PATTI RELIVES THE FIRE OVER AND OVER. The smell of trout that drove her from the kitchen. She will always despise fish.

Maybe it was because pregnancy was already like getting sea legs, the feeling of grasping after a new centre of gravity, but the smell of the fish was like brine and blood choking her throat. Like the feeling of her tongue on an oxidized chain, an anchor being dragged up out of her belly, dark orange and furred with barnacles. Saline and foam in her mouth turning to bile.

Patti ran to the bathroom, so close to the kitchen that the sinks shared a drainpipe. The kitchen sink was full of two largish pots soaking clean. She left the bathroom door open and the children as they were, Ryan colouring at the kitchen table, chattering to Clara, who sat in the playpen near the back door. Hurrying to the toilet, she lowered herself to her knees and took a moment, maybe ten seconds, to use both hands to hold back the loose front curls of dark red hair from where they hung about her face.

This day was the day that Patti was late to start supper because she'd wasted an hour trying to get pretty, darting in and out of the bedroom to struggle into clothes that didn't fit, swiping at hair that had fallen limp in the humidity. When she realized the time, she made fast work of dinner, putting on rice and green beans and chocolate pudding. Three out of four burners. Trout in the oven.

As she vomited she thought, it was all for nothing. She would be clammy and pale when he got home. Too dejected to feel sexy.

It was a strange, shrill cry that she heard, vaguely feline, and for a disorienting moment Patti thought she was hearing the baby inside her.

She reached the kitchen just as Ryan was setting

Clara down on the floor, yelping as he backed away. It took Patti a moment to see the flames at Clara's wrist and only a second later they were running across Clara's back and into her hair and everything about Clara was changing colour before her eyes. Patti grabbed the biggest pot soaking in the sink and threw the water over her daughter, and then again with the second pot before pushing her to the floor, covering her with her body and rolling with her. She was screaming no, no, no, no, no, no, no. Clara screamed, too, but not in words.

The story, as far as it could be reconstructed from Ryan's terrified retelling, was that Clara wanted to taste the pudding. Patti had sometimes offered Ryan a lick off her spoon as she stirred a dessert, heating it slowly on the stove.

It started with Ryan finding Clara her baby spoon and heaving her up toward the stovetop. Like David, he has always been strong. As Clara aimed for the pudding pot, the sleeve of her nightgown drooped down into the gas flame.

DAVID SAYS, IT'S NOT YOUR FAULT. Rocking her like a baby. He tells her, I don't blame you. Don't blame yourself. It was an accident. He puts his hand in her hair and rubs her scalp.

Patti cries and cries. She hates crying because she looks ugly. She is shocked that this awareness hasn't left her, even at such a moment. She says, I hate myself.

David says, I love you.

PATTI USED TO THINK, THIS IS LIVING. This is what life is made of. This while drinking wine in the park, or going out for dinner with her last twenty dollars, eating spicy noodles until her nose ran clear, eyes streaming. Riding the night bus to New York City for a free rock show. Making love, even before she quite figured out how to enjoy it. These were the important things, the ones worth sacrificing for. The way to make memories. The way to feel.

Then came a time when she told herself this about pregnancy, the quickening, labour itself, the matchless feeling of suckling her babies at her breast. Now as she goes from room to room, gathering an unwholesome harvest of dirty clothes, she wonders what generative force has worked this transformation, skewed her ranking of values until they seem as though they might belong to somebody else.

She thinks, I'd like to go back.

It was something about Ryan turning up, rousing in her a kind of vying covetousness. When she'd hinted, David had only hummed.

I guess you want me to give you a baby, he said with his hick twang. He kissed her hard, reaching up under her shirt, pressing himself against her as though willing to undertake it right then.

Sometimes she tries to distance herself from the woman who birthed them, the swollen woman who wept with anxiety, wore sweatpants, lined their bedrooms with wallpaper trim in patterns of bunnies or spaceships. From the kind of woman who ever thought to care about trim.

Under her feet, she can feel the Levis David sloughed off the night before. He sometimes undresses in the laundry room, a perfect instance of the concision of his nature. Preternaturally succinct in all things, shockingly so, she thinks, for a writer, but what does she know. Before tossing them into the wash, she fishes through the pockets and finds his wedding band, a cool circle of white gold. She holds it in her hand for a moment before placing it on the shelf above the washer. After a moment, she changes her mind and brings it to the bedroom, setting it down on his bedside table where she has seen him put it at night.

She sets about collecting the next load of laundry, mostly the loose, cotton items she buys for Clara, the recommended clothing for burn victims. It is still important to keep her skin safe from the sun. As she sorts her daughter's clothes into the basket, Patti thinks of Clara's grafts, how the doctors took from one part of her to heal another. But the places that hurt Clara the most throughout everything were those parts that they cut away, the good bits of skin from her bottom and from her thighs that would grow again on their own without leaving any marks. The good parts that were turned into something else, into the raspberry stains they hope will fade. And Patti considers this and thinks that there is no trace left now of who she herself was before, the parts of her made over into this married woman with kids. The only one who shows.

THE LAST NIGHT IN THE OLD HOUSE David takes the kids over to Jan's at seven o'clock. They are celebrating. David had an idea of making dinner for Paul and his wife, one of Patti's fancy desserts and his meditative pea risotto, but Patti pointed out that their pots and dishes have been packed, the house a waiting reliquary of boxes, so they are going to an Italian restaurant downtown.

For some reason, everyone orders osso buco, even Patti, who is usually turned off by the sight of bone protruding from her meal. She is distracted, floating just above the flow of the conversation. David and Paul play at a hearty dispute over who is to buy the wine, and they end up getting two bottles, both red.

David says, it looks like it's going to be that kind of night.

Paul says, good Lord, don't you have to get up early for the movers?

They all laugh. Patti thinks, it looks like it's going to be that kind of night. Endless goodwill and merriment. She gulps at her wine, anxious about her own unease.

We'll be neighbours now, says Paul. We'll be borrowing sugar right and left.

Do you like babysitting? asks Patti. Paul says, sure, but Patti sees him shoot a nervous look first at David, who shakes his head, then at his wife, who only smiles.

She looks at Paul's wife, Jessica, and thinks that she is beautiful. She is seated across from David, as Patti sits opposite Paul. She has long, black hair and an exotic mouth glossed to a dark pink. Patti drops her fork on purpose to check that no one's legs are touching.

You'll have to get a new one, says David, giving her a close look. His voice, to Patti, sounds reproving. She shrugs.

When the wine comes, David fills everyone's glasses and suggests a round of toasts.

To the future, says Jessica.

To freedom, says David.

To justice, says Paul.

To love, Patti says.

As Patti clinks everyone's glasses, taking a moment to lock eyes according to the new adage, she scans for guilt or betrayal. And in everyone's gaze, every flicker of light and moisture in the eye, she sees only bluster, and perhaps kindness, and a trace of something like her own helpless puzzlement staring back.

Look, But Don't Touch

"Look, but don't touch," I say.

My mouth is dry and my words are charged with the buzz of constant instruction. I hold Brian's hand, stand between him and the sombre gallery guard, whose age-stricken face might activate my brother's potent sense of terror. He is still tense from the scene at the coat-check counter where they forced him to turn in his new disposable camera. Whispering soft in his ear, I rub the small of his back, affixing the shiny orange visitor's tag to the top of his shirt pocket. He fingers it, rubbing its smooth metal surface with his left thumb, his throat gurgling in a tuneless hum.

I let go of his hand, linking my elbow around his right

arm and steering him toward the entrance to the European Gallery. I like to walk this way with my younger brother, dwarfed by his solid mass, yet gently, almost indiscernibly, in control.

Almost nothing in his face singles him out as different. There is a slight pucker in his pink lips and sometimes, behind the wire frames of his glasses, his eyes look searching and anxious. But really, whose don't? His dark hair is soft and straight and, if left to its own devices, falls forward over his face in a fringe that makes him look younger than his nineteen years. His tongue is larger than normal. He's double-jointed. And he has small ears, small and perfect like a china doll's.

All this to say that he has an extra chromosome, but I don't really know what that means. When I was six years old and my parents brought him home from the hospital, I used to look for it, peeling back the layers of soft flannel and examining every inch of his round, pink body.

Without my arm prompting him to place one foot in front of the other, Brian would be standing here motionless, eyes wide. We are stopped in front of a portrait of a woman. Her hair is blonde and fine, painted in painstaking detail in the Flemish tradition.

"She's a pretty girl," says Brian. His free hand travels toward his crotch but I swat it away.

I stop us in front of a Van Gogh. The hypergreen leaves at the base of the iris thrive and threaten. The grass is electrified, jutting upwards in viscous dabs. I remember how I used to long to touch all the canvases, map the images under my fingers. And I see Brian's free arm swinging upwards, hands reaching out toward the painting. I stop him in time, pin his arms at his side, but the security guard is already at our backs. I break into the harsh torrent of his words.

"*Pardon, pardon. Mon frère, il ne comprend pas.*"

The guard, hearing my accent, switches to English with the official-language courtesy so typical to Ottawa.

"If your brother does not understand not to touch the paintings, *mademoiselle*, he will have to leave the gallery."

Brian is whimpering. I am holding his wrists now, in a way that is probably uncomfortable for him.

"I'll make sure he doesn't touch any more." I nod down toward his hands, limp within my grip. "And I'll make sure we stand far back from all the paintings."

The guard looks at us. My flushed cheeks and Brian's tearful pout. He nods.

"*D'accord.*"

As I lead Brian away to the next room, I see the guard speaking into his walkie-talkie. His mouth brushes the speaker and I shudder at this sterile intimacy. Brian's wrists are moist and still trembling within my grasp.

MY MOTHER IS CLEANING THE KITCHEN, scrubbing the inside of the stove because her sister is coming to visit. She's been to the hairdresser so she is wearing a butterfly-print shower cap over her fresh blonde curls. I am cleaning the kitchen too, kneeling on the floor and scrubbing wide arcs with my pink rubber gloves. My mother insists upon both my help and the necessity of what she calls saving my hands. Addressing me with her face still in the oven, her voice echoing and tinny, she asks me to fold up the massage table that I keep upstairs in the sun room where I do treatments on my clients.

"It looks messy, Kate," she says, "having it right in the middle of the room like that."

"It's the only thing in the room," I say. "It can't be messy if it's the only thing." The only thing except for the plants on the sills and two floating shelves that hold a small array of candles and oils. An oasis compared to the clutter of my bedroom, where clothes and books contend for the most floor space.

My mother rises and turns to rinse her sponge at the sink. "You know what I mean. Don't you remember the way your Aunt Sylvia keeps house?"

It is at least twelve years since our last family visit out west to see Aunt Sylvia and Uncle Matthew. "Of course not. I barely even remember their house. All I remember is playing with Hannah on her swing set. And Brian splashing around in their little kiddie pool."

I also remember the sunshine of the fenced back yard, the memory a thirty-second movie reel of happiness. A distinct sense of safety and freedom in knowing Brian was completely surrounded by people who understood him and loved him.

I straighten up from my position on the floor after a final swipe and my mother looks at me and says, "You need to clean your room. Aren't you tired of me telling you that? And please weed the garden when you're done."

"I'll clean it," I say, starting to leave. Even two years ago, this same conversation would have ended in a yelling match reminiscent of my high school days. It is an old routine, and I don't blame my mother for feeling exasperated. She probably didn't expect to have two children who would never leave home.

I CAN TELL THAT MY CLIENT holds me in contempt a little because I work out of my home, but he comes to me because he is cheap and my rates are lower than at the clinic. He has dark, curling hair, greying over the ears. It is nice hair, and when he is face-down on my table I can almost imagine he is a good-looking man.

He is lying naked under a white sheet. His head and shoulders are visible and that is where I begin, working downward from the top of his body. His flesh feels soft and gives me a pessimistic feeling about the human body. It is so quick to lose its pliancy, to begin its slide into excess. Most of my clients are middle-aged men whose balance of tissue has slipped from their chests to their waists like a doughy life preserver.

His pale skin always surprises me with its coolness, and I begin briskly so that I can watch the colour flow into the parts I have worked on. By the time I reach his lower back, there are warm patches of red above his shoulder blades. I stare at my hands, at their long, freckled skinniness, as the man continues to let out quiet moans under their touch.

I reflect that this kind of contact is a poor substitute for intimacy, although this client is not one of the ones who come for that reason. What I do is more akin to the emptying-out of intimacy, to the point where I am like a machine to this man. If there were an affordable mechanical substitute, I would never see him again.

At the base of his spine, I fold back the sheet. Fine,

dark hairs cover his buttocks, which I knead like dough, feeling the knots of tension loosen and dissipate. Although he never speaks to me, I know that this is the seat of his stress and of his occupation. He sits all day at work, telling people things they do not want to hear. He makes the most noise during this part of the massage—soft, muted groans of pleasure—and a sigh of relief escapes my own lips as I move on to his upper thighs.

As I replace the sheet over his buttocks, I think of my college classes, full of bright, practical girls whose hands must now have touched thousands of naked bodies. I wish I could experience one of my own massages. Would I even like it? Since getting my certificate, I have only worked on clients, never friends, and I am never sure whether my clients and I haven't become confused about the difference between pleasure and pain.

MARIA, THE COMMUNITY-CARE WORKER, smiles at me when I arrive and touches Brian on his shoulder. He turns and waves, his wet hair dripping water down his face. Maria and Brian are the two oldest people in the outdoor pool, and the younger kids are giving them a wide berth, possibly because Brian has never yet lost a splashing contest.

I watch them get out of the pool, and Maria folds a

red towel around Brian's shoulders. She wraps herself in a blue one and waits as I walk Brian to the male change room in the community centre. Brian is good at dressing himself, as long as somebody else picks out his clothes. Otherwise he would try to wear his khaki shorts even in the winter.

Beside the pool, Maria pulls a sundress over her yellow bathing suit and wrings out her long, dark braid.

"I hate chlorine," she says, swinging her hair back in a spray of droplets and smiling at me.

"Me, too. How was Brian today?"

"Wonderful. He's a water baby, that one."

"You got that right."

"How was your client?"

"Oh. Fine. You know."

"You know, anytime you need me, I can take Brian for you."

"Oh. Thanks. That's nice. That's good to know."

At the park, after Maria leaves, I buy us Robo Pops and we sit together on a bench under a shady tree. I read as Brian watches a man and a dog playing Frisbee close by. By the time we have both eaten down to the blue sections on our popsicles, the man and the dog have been replaced by a group of girls sitting on a grey blanket they have spread out on the grass. One of them, the tallest, is very beautiful, and her turquoise flounced skirt falls back as she bends her long leg to paint her toenails. I hear a loud slurping sound and look over to see Brian pulling the blue popsicle stick from his mouth, his eyes intent on the lounging teens.

"She's a pretty girl," he says, loud enough for them to hear. "She's a pretty girl, but I'm not allowed to touch her."

The girls are staring at us when I grab Brian by the arm and start leading him home. The girl in the blue skirt has tucked her legs underneath her by the time we pass by.

"Look, but don't touch," says Brian.

"Sorry," I mutter.

BRIAN WILL GO TO BED BY HIMSELF as long as he has a goodnight hug. Our house is cold at night, even in the summer, and my nipples are hard against his chest as he hugs me. I feel the swelling in his pants turn to stone against my groin. I lean into it, for a moment, before I pull away.

The potency of Brian's body is bitter to me in its incongruence. I remember my own body betraying me into sexuality, my breasts rounded secrets under my sweaters in the playground. My brother's vigorous physicality is delivering a summons he is unable to heed.

I try to imagine a purely physical ecstasy, a bare instinct instead of recycled fantasies. Thought flowing from sensation as it would for Brian, as it must have for everyone before the eating of the fruit or the advent of the frontal lobe. I think about touching him, meeting him on the navy blue of his bedspread, and the quick release that would follow. The simple pleasure of my kind, strong brother. His happiness in my hands, for a moment.

But it is important not to touch him. In his innocence, it would become like the ice cream, the video-games, for which he clamours day and night.

THERE IS ONLY ONE DAY LEFT before my relatives arrive. I am helping my mother dust all of the downstairs and avoiding the weeding that awaits me in the garden. Brian is helping me, making the process both longer and more enjoyable. In our system, he trails after me holding either the polish and the rag or the feather duster, whichever I'm not using, and keeps up a constant stream of questions about his cousin Hannah.

"Is Hannah as pretty as you, Katie?"

"Much prettier." I show him the snapshot taped into their last Christmas card, still standing on the top of our piano—my mother always holds on to family Christmas cards until the new ones arrive. In the photo, Uncle Matthew and Aunt Sylvia stand to either side of Hannah, posed in front of their fireplace. Hannah is a few years younger than we are, with a bright, even smile and friendly eyes. Her red knit sweater brings out the glow of her blonde hair.

"Hannah is a music student," I say. "She plays the flute."

"What's the flute?" He frowns as I run the feather duster along the case of the piano covering the keys.

"You remember, Brian. It's that long silver instrument that sounds like a girl singing." I look at him and he shakes his head.

"Remember when we learned all the instruments?" Then Brian nods, biting his lower lip.

"She'll probably bring it with her," I tell him, "so maybe she'll show it to you."

"Because she's my cousin?"

"Yes. She's your cousin."

"My cousin. And yours, too. Right, Katie?"

I brush his hair off his forehead. "That's right." I replace the picture in its card on the piano, and Brian turns his attention to the other ornaments decorating its surface. His hands hover over a blown glass vase, one of my mother's treasures.

"Don't touch, Brian," I say automatically.

"Okay," he says, staring at its swirling pinks and yellows. He looks back at me.

"Maria has fourteen cousins," he says. "Why does she have so many?"

"Some people have more than others," I tell him. I kiss him on the forehead the way I always do when I feel that I have told him something profound about life. He scratches at the spot where my lips moistened his skin, then wanders toward the kitchen.

"Let's have ice cream," he calls out.

HANNAH AND AUNT SYLVIA are finishing off the last tiny pieces of pound cake and my mother delights in pouring more tea for me and her sister. I am nervous that Brian will want to partake of this ritual, imperilling my mother's blue-and-white china, but he turns up his nose at it, instead marking the occasion by indulging in ice cream at lunchtime. It is Neapolitan, as always, and he shovels it from a plastic orange bowl in heaping spoonfuls.

Hannah is tinier than I would have guessed from her pictures, a full head shorter than me. Everything about her seems delicate and sweet. Against the edge of the table, her wrists seem barely larger than the butter spreader. When she excuses herself, she asks Brian if he would like to show her the yard, where Uncle Matthew is mowing the lawn. Brian looks at me.

"Go ahead," I say, and my mother and Aunt Sylvia give noisy and pleased assent.

"Just don't let Brian into the garden," says my mother. "He'll trample the flowers."

"Hannah is so good with children," says Aunt Sylvia, as we watch my cousin lead Brian away.

"Brian isn't a child," I say, as I begin to clear the largest platter.

"Oh, I know, dear," says Aunt Sylvia. She turns to my mother. "I just mean she has such a way with her. People respond to her."

My mother sips her tea, nodding with enthusiasm.

"Oh, yes. She's certainly grown into a lovely girl." She looks at me. "You were all so small the last time you played together."

I nod before I head toward the sink with the platter and the used napkins. When I look outside, I can see Hannah pulling Brian away from the garden's neat border of flat, pink granite, and Uncle Matt waving them over to see a blue jay in the maple, just about to take flight.

UNCLE MATT AND AUNT SYLVIA are driving downtown to go shopping, and Hannah and Brian are going with them. All four of them are up and ready to go before I'm out of my pyjamas. When I return from the kitchen with a cup of coffee, my mother is gathering scattered sections of the newspaper into a single pile. At the door, Brian zips himself into his red windbreaker with a look of glee.

"You can't come with us today, Katie," he tells me. "We're giving you a little *break*."

He makes it sound like a hardship, like a punch in the ribs or a surprise trip to the dentist.

"Uh-oh," I say. "Poor me."

"Poor you," he agrees. "You have to have a break."

"That's right, Brian," says Aunt Sylvia. "Kate deserves a day off." She sounds louder than normal, looking harried as she digs through her purse for the car keys. Uncle Matt ducks his head and starts tapping his toe. Hannah is squeezing a black flute case between her knees as she threads her arms into a long camel sweater. The day promises to be hot, but everyone is dressed for air conditioning.

"It's just that we want to spend some time with you, Brian," says Hannah. "This is our day together." She pulls loose her hair then grabs the case by its handle. It's covered in stickers, sparkly pinks and purples, stars and hearts and bears. She turns her face up to Brian's.

"Right?" she says. I like the way she looks at Brian without glancing at me first, or afterward.

"I know," he says. "It's our day. I have a lot of things I want us to do at the mall." Brian has his hand on the doorknob, turning it back and forth in a racket of clicking. "Katie has to stay home this time."

"Too bad for me," I say. "You guys have fun."

When everyone is gone, my mother spins into action—a whirlwind of tidying with me as the eye, the still centre running along the same trajectory but touching nothing.

"We did all this two days ago," I say, but she ignores me.

Instead, she steers us onto the subject of Hannah and her good grades, her pretty hair, her first-place finish in the Kiwanis festival. "I'm so happy Hannah is coming out on the other side of high school as such a good, smart girl." She says this as though adolescence is a trial by fire, or a stint in the big house. Dipping a sheet of newsprint into a vinegar-and-water solution, she rinses toothpaste splatter from the bathroom mirror. Brian is energetic about brushing his teeth. My mother wrinkles her nose at her reflection. By the time we hit the spare room, she is quizzing me on whether or not she looks older than her sister.

"I don't know," I say. "You *are* older, right?" I blink at the hospital corners she has made on the guest bed with its shrimp-pink sheets, neat creases on each side like badges of compliance. They remind me of the way Brian prefers his sandwiches, slices of ham tucked strictly within the bounds of the bread, every rogue edge trimmed, and I realize it must be almost lunchtime. "I guess you do have more grey hair."

"Oh, you're not even looking," she says. "Here, do something." She thrusts one side of the bedspread at me and together we draw it up over the pillows. "You know she dyes hers. She must. It used to be sepia and now it's like a raw umber."

My mother has never abandoned her vocabulary from our crayon colouring days, a habit I find touching.

"Yes, I think you might be right."

Later, she pulls out the ledger.

"Budget day," she says. I bring down a yogourt container full of money from the massage business. Room and board. She pulls out the drawer with the utility bills, the bank statements, and the stubs from Brian's disability cheques.

"Find me a pencil," she says.

She counts out twenties, punches in numbers, smoothes out the wadded currency into a face-up stack.

The adding machine whirrs and spits out our tally in a long white tongue, a defiant expression of survival. She is starting on next month's projections when everyone arrives home. Brian bounds in ahead of my aunt and uncle, Hannah close behind him.

"Guess what," he says. "We went busking. Hannah played her flute and I danced and people clapped for me." He is so delighted he can hardly speak, his eagerness choking off the ends of his words. A fleck of spit catches on his lip. "And people gave us money. Lots and lots and lots." He has his hand in his pocket and I can hear the clinking of change.

"What?" demands my mother. She pulls her glasses down on her nose, and Brian freezes. He knows her expressions as well as I do. Hannah clears her throat, but I cut in.

"Was it fun?" I ask.

"Oh yeah!" Brian turns in my direction, relieved. I can see two dark sweat patches on his shirt that have already begun to dry.

"Okay, then." I fend off the image of a crowd gathering, teenage boys egging him on. Anybody at all laughing in the wrong way. The scenario, I have a feeling, our mother already deems a certainty. "That's great."

"Everyone was having a good time," says Hannah.

She looks at me and then at my mother, who slams the ledger back in its drawer and heads to the living room. Hannah blushes.

"I didn't realize Brian was such a dancer," she says. "He was trying to take everyone for a spin."

Brian looks smug. "I danced with three girls," he says, and in a way I am glad I wasn't there to stop him.

HANNAH FEELS BAD, I CAN TELL. She has been at my elbow all evening, asking questions, whispering confidences, fixing me in a shy smile as she twirls her fingers in the ends of her hair. Settled at the end of my bed, she holds out her hands.

"See my nails?" she says. "Mum pays for me to get manicures."

I inspect them, their rose-hued sheen and pearly tips. "Professional expense," says Hannah. "I used to bite them."

She turns my palms down and looks at my nails, cut short and squarish.

"It's better for not jabbing the clients," I say. "Until I started cutting them I had one guy who begged for back scratches. And he had acne."

"Ew, ew. Oh, gross." Hannah rocks back on her heels, face scrunched in disgust and delight. She tells me

I'm a healer.

"It's one of the great callings," she says. "Healer, artist, teacher." She has already confided her ten-year plan, which includes securing a first chair in a major orchestra and offering free music lessons to underprivileged kids.

"Nice how you've managed to fit us both on the list," I say.

"I'm serious. When did you know it was what you wanted to do?"

My shrugging around Hannah is almost a given. Her earnestness floors me. I just shake my head, but I gather she's used to getting answers to her questions. She seems younger than seventeen, more sensitive, or maybe just more candid. Her face falls, and she says, "You think I'm lame."

"No, of course not."

"I got a massage, once. Last year before my competition." She jumps up and says, "One sec."

When she comes back in she is holding a bottle of massage oil.

"Why don't you teach me how? We'll practice on Brian."

WE DECIDE TO DO IT IN MY BEDROOM since the noise of setting up the massage table might attract the attention of our parents. I close the door and turn up the heat. Hannah pulls away the thin mattress of the rollaway cot she's been sleeping on and lays it on the floor. I go to the sunroom to retrieve my textbook with the biggest diagrams.

When I come back I see that Hannah has stripped down to her underwear, a pink tank top and matching shorts.

"Hot in here," she says.

"It's best for the muscles," I say. "I'll get Brian."

When Brian is prone on the mattress, his pyjama top removed and chuckles mostly suppressed, I show Hannah how to do pressure strokes along the base of the spine, how to knead the shoulders with the heels of her hands. I remember, suddenly, my mother massaging Brian when he was a baby, stimulating his small limbs with the hope of improving his poor muscle tone.

"Maybe I should have been doing this all along," I say aloud. "Good idea."

When Brian complains of being thirsty, I volunteer to get us all some water. With the heat on, the air is dry. Downstairs, my mother is looking for a new CD to put on.

"Are you guys playing Monopoly up there?" asks Aunt Sylvia. The evening's suggested activity.

"Not quite. We're having fun, though."

When I get upstairs, I see that Brian has turned over and Hannah is straddling him. Her hands are on his bare chest and he has one hand on her arm, the other moving up under the side of her top. She is laughing in gasps as though she is being tickled. Then she bobs down so her hair is in his face and she kisses his neck.

"Hannah," I say, and Brian pulls down and squeezes her very hard. When she cries out, I am not sure if it because he is hurting her or because she has spotted our mothers behind me.

"Katherine," says my mother. "What's going on?"

Aunt Sylvia just steps in and starts screaming at my brother.

Hannah gets up, and there is a bright red handprint on her arm above her elbow. She rubs at it.

"Don't be mad," she says, and I have no idea who she's talking to. Brian's face crumples. He is sitting up now, twisting the waistband of his pyjama pants in his fingers.

"You never said I couldn't," he says to me. "You said she was my cousin. Mine."

IN THE EARLY MORNING, AFTER THE OTHERS have left with tight-lipped and discomfited goodbyes, we sit together in the garden. We have pulled off our shoes and our feet press into the dark moistness of the dirt as we crouch together above the neat rows of flowers. Brian is silent and still terrified. He keeps looking over his shoulder as though he expects to see our mother or our aunt scolding him. After the first explosion, when Hannah continued to declare that she was fine, my mother sent Brian to his room. Then, with Aunt Sylvia, she went downstairs to keep arguing. Hannah and I went to bed in silence, listening to their furious exchange.

"Like this," I say, closing his hand over the top of a weed and drawing it back until he has pulled it out by the roots.

When my mother returns, we are still in the garden, our hands tired and blistered and covered with dirt.

The Beater

ONE OF YOUR EARLIEST MEMORIES is of your mother hurrying you down the street, telling you not to look at your house. You circle the block, hand in hand, until the man who has followed you off the bus turns down the next street. Her whisper is a hissing shriek: "It's him, it's him. Don't look. We can't let him know where we live."

You stumble to keep up, legs trembling. You're three, and fear is contagious. Inside, she pushes a chair against the double-bolted door, draws the curtains, and takes you into her lap to say the rosary. The beads, smooth and black, brush against your cheek until it tickles.

You didn't know who he was then. He was just a bad man. One of that black-hearted vanguard of purposeless evil, the bad men. The ones you had to watch out for because they might lure you with candy or grab you in a supermarket. They might even know your name.

WHEN SHE TOLD YOU, she was emotional and you were uncomfortable in a way that you learned later was called embarrassment. You sat with one leg under you on the beloved yellow footstool by the window, its corduroy rubbed bare in the centre. Playing with the one remaining tassel as you watched her features reddening, her expression blurring into sorrow.

Her version of the story was almost unbelievable in its simplicity. Before you and your father, before he took off and left, there was another man. A bad man. A beater. They had three children, and then she ran away. Her voice broke as you pressed for the details, her grey-streaked blonde hair clinging to her hangdog cheeks. What were their names? How old were they now? This was when she said, "Don't make me talk about it." And so you didn't, not then. You didn't like seeing her cry.

NEW PEOPLE HAVE MOVED IN NEXT DOOR. Their door is open as you let yourself into your apartment, and you catch a glimpse of a mattress and a moulded plastic chair. A man rocks in its seat, one huge boot against the wall as a brace, laces untied and skimming the floor. On a milk crate sits a television set with almost no reception, the frantic black-and-white static swirling with patches of colour, the sound obscured by a loud buzzing. It reminds you of your mother vacuuming up the gravelly bits of stray cat litter, the machine roaring to life with a faint smoky smell, the furious rattling of everything it consumed.

You notice a woman on the mattress as she stirs and reaches forward to turn up the volume. The man on the chair lets loose a laugh like a hoarse bark and your stomach jumps. A baby, somewhere in another room, is crying.

Slipping inside, you lock the door behind you. Back in 1900, this was a luxury building, just down the street from the Legislature on a wide and empty Broadway, and the two adjacent apartments were only one. Later, as the prospects of the grand avenue faltered along with the hopes of the city, the huge apartment was split unevenly into two, your front unit retaining the fireplace and bay windows, the other backing onto it like a small storage locker. Divided along lines of fortune, just like the rest of the world.

THERE ARE NO PHOTOGRAPHS OF THEM in your mother's bedroom. You searched it so many times, knees burning from the rub of the carpet as you slid open drawer after drawer. Pushing aside the carefully folded sweaters and slacks, lifting up the paper lining spread flat along the bottom panel—wrapping-paper from your baby presents, patterned with teddy bears and rocking horses, still bright ten years later. You searched, too, the cedar chest at the foot of her bed when you found it unlocked, but there was only a silver cup, a Girl Guide handkerchief, and a boxful of slides from a car trip with your father, a bell-bottomed redbeard at her side in twenty-eight states, as lanky and aquiline-nosed as you. Stationery from Universal Studios. A crumbling fur hat shedding fox hair from a pelt like a dried husk. Mementos of things that happened before the beater, and after.

There is just one black-and-white photograph of your mother, skinnier than you have ever seen her, squinting in a flowered sundress in front of a house you don't recognize. Caught in the edge of the picture is a man turned away, dark hair glinting in the light. You can see only one thick arm, doubled up like a hoisted pennant as he scratches the back of his neck. You think, *That's him.*

You used to think of the three children as the lost babies. The lost little ones. You still sometimes catch yourself doing it. It is a strange kind of pathos to attach to people who would by now be nearly forty.

———

THE DOORBELL RINGS, and against your own instinct, you answer it. Your mother would call you a fool if she knew. "That's the way they get you," she said, one night over the phone. "Home invaders. I saw it on the news. They just ring the doorbell and when you answer it they conk you over the head and rob you blind. Or rape you and murder you and take all your stuff."

Your mother never opens the front door unless she sees through the peephole that it is a small child. Even then, sometimes not.

"They'll just be selling something," she used to say, so close to the door you were sure they could hear. "Do they think I'm made of money?"

The woman at the door has bleached blonde hair, the brown roots growing out in a dark furrow across her scalp. You find yourself frowning as though at your own reflection, as though finding fault with the image you project. Her ponytail is rumpled at the side, blonde strands pulled loose and wreathing her head like a halo, and you reach up a hand to smooth your own fair hair back behind your ears. She exhales, her mouth broadened into a smile, but her body stiffens and her shoulders twist as she prepares to speak. There are many people in the world who are capable of feeling disappointment just by looking at you, and it seems she is one of them. But you're not sure why.

"Hi, I'm Michelle," she says. She has a lean baby on her hip, his head resting against her chest, blue eyes solemn and alert. "I just moved in next door, so I guess we're neighbours. I was wondering if I could borrow some plates. And some forks and knives and stuff."

"Uh, sure," you say, extending your hand to take hold of her chapped palm as she heaves the silent baby farther up with her left arm. "Lucy. I think I might have a couple extras."

You want to tell her it isn't possible for you to help her, want to show her the cupboards of Kraft Dinner, the used textbooks, the baseboards furred with dust. The thousands of little indicators that ought to be proof enough that you can barely help yourself.

She grins and you notice tiny, crooked teeth. They give her thin smile an almost winsome look.

"Thanks," she says. "I'll wait here."

YOUR MOTHER HAS A BINDER full of bus schedules for every bus from 1 to 87. She spreads them across the table when you come to visit, fresh off an overnight train from the west. Pressed flat within plastic sleeves, their columns of arrival times are bordered with neatly pencilled marginalia. You notice dates and times, notes colour-coded in different inks. Here and there, names and other details. Beside a morning bus, the 50, she has written *Justin. Bought $70,000 truck.*

"What on earth is this?"

Your mother looks. "Oh, that's Justin," she says. "He just bought a $70,000 truck."

When you keep staring, her cheeks bulge a little in exasperation. "He's the bus driver. I take that bus every day to work. We chat."

More often the notes say things like *Five minutes late Dec. 5* or *Wheelchair-enabled bus daily since Apr. 27.* Your mother is not in a wheelchair, but she is always looking forward in gloom, anticipating future horrors. She has already asked your Uncle Billy how much it would cost to have safety bars installed around the toilet, to help her get up and down. Every time she eats a sweet she says, "I might as well enjoy this. I'll probably have diabetes by next year."

Half your mother's phone conversations revolve around the flaws and successes of the transit system in relation to her trips around the city, and the people she has met while taking the bus. But it seems to be a more all-consuming preoccupation than you had imagined.

She grabs the binder out of your hands, huffy.

"I thought you'd be impressed. I spent a lot of time

on it." She tilts her head with a touch of resentful pride. "You know, with this, I never get stuck out on the street in the dark. I never have to wait alone."

She is angry that you moved away from her to go to school. She says, "Without you, I have nobody."

AT HOME, YOU TYPE THEIR NAMES OVER and over, hoping for some sort of connection to catapult them toward you, to beam you a signal from the tangled masses of data. Maybe from a Peterborough accounting firm, or a Moncton secondary school, or a trailer park registry in North Dakota. The mantra of their given names is your accompaniment as your fingers clatter over the keyboard.

It was long before the days of search engines when your mother finally said them aloud. Christopher, Mary, Annette. The cadence of your questioning keeps time with the clicking of the mouse. Where are you? Where are you? And what have you become?

You think they must have been one of the last generations of people whose names aren't splashed across the internet, littering pages here and there with piecemeal versions of their lives and interests. An award here, an office telephone listing there. An emotional outpouring on a Rush fan message board. It seems almost impossible to get lost nowadays. But the two girls, her girls, would have married, their last names vanished, peeled back like fraying threads from family ties, from any safety rope you could try to grab hold of.

YOU CAN HEAR VOICES through your bookcase, pitched to the shrill tones of conflict. When the neighbours fight, your ears perk up. You move away from the computer, pull down the books from the shelves, piling them onto the floor in thick stacks until the conversation emerges in muffled bursts.

"I know you cashed that cheque—"

"...they keep calling..."

"Lena thinks... worthless... sick."

A television show plays in the background, blaring a nasty interview, and its stagey, predictable dialogue competes for your attention. Everything you hear through the wall sounds like a talk show, like dysfunctional family members lunging at each other over stage set chairs.

There is a thump like the sound of something falling, but just then you knock over a stack of books. It tips as you lean closer to the other apartment, books tumbling to the floor, scattering and sliding under the desk, the futon, and the radiator, which gurgles and spits as it heats, as though contemptuous of any human need for warmth.

Before you can gather the books, you hear someone

shout, "Let go!" and for a moment you are afraid. But then you think that it could have been "Let's go!" and when you hear their door slam shut you feel relieved as you curl up on the futon, letting the blather of their television soothe you to sleep, each bout of shouted re-criminations like the next verse in a lullaby.

YOUR MOTHER IS TALKING, deploring the price of green grapes, even before you have the phone up to your ear.

"I nearly died when they came to eight dollars," she says. "It's highway robbery. But I have to buy them. They cheer me up. I eat a bag every two days."

"It's no wonder your stomach is always upset," you say. One of your mother's usual remarks. You remember her telling you that any more than fourteen grapes at a time would give you the runs.

"They're fine," she says. Why do you always have to put down everything I'm excited about? Sometimes I think you're not a very nice person."

Her voice sounds tremulous on the phone, but when pushed, she will become petulant. She has always been this way, her shows of weakness turning to flashes of irritation and spite. She lets out a loud sigh.

"I've been really depressed today," she says. "I think I might be bipolar."

"Where did you hear about bipolar?"

"You're not the only one who knows about things, you know."

"I know."

You think of the lost children, in a flash, as you listen to your mother on the phone. Your ear hot and moist with sweat, you think they might have gotten off easy.

MICHELLE LOOKS TIRED. The red in her eyes is matched by pink spots on her face, surrounding the base of her nose and running along the edge of her chin, as though her old skin is wearing away in patches, in a disorganized sloughing. She looks thinner than before, too, her arms slight and stringy beneath a grey tank top. You can hear the reedy cry of the baby from the other room.

"Yeah?" she says. Then, turning her head, she shouts, "Will you do something to make Christopher shut up? Please?" Nobody answers, but the howling gets louder. You notice an odd tremor in your legs as you register the name.

"Is he named after his father?" you ask. "The baby?"

"What?" says Michelle. "No. What do you want?"

"It's my plates," you say. "I need them back." With every overheard fight, you feel the retrieval of your stuff becoming less and less likely. Though you often hear them coming and going, it has been a month since you've seen Michelle face to face.

She frowns. "Wait here."

She returns with half of the plates you gave her. Neither of you says anything about the cutlery. She thrusts the dishes into your hands.

"There," she says. Her eyebrows are raised as though this were the latest in a series of bizarre demands.

"Thanks so much," you gush, but your smile only elicits another eyebrow twitch, a pressing together of the lips that is not a smile, and a nod as she closes the door.

YOUR MOTHER SAYS HE THREW THE BABY against the wall. She says, "You have no idea. He beat me up and one time when he was drunk he threw the baby against the wall." She says the baby instead of Christopher, which you know was the name of the youngest one. You have never heard her say their names aloud, except for that one time you asked, determined you would never forget. Although you wonder if she sometimes says them out loud to herself, or in dreams that might contribute to her fits of temper and sudden lows.

She tells you this so that you will understand her terror, her justification for running away from everything she had ever known, for weighing both of your lives down with regret. But you can only think of what the beater would have done had he been left alone with the baby, which you picture as just a little shaken after making contact with the wall, a bit cross, eyes squeezed shut and howling. You remember wondering as a child what it would take for your mother to leave you, and thinking, "Is that all?"

In truth, there is no real way for you to picture a baby hitting the wall. It's always a pillow, a rag doll. Nothing that could really break.

Maybe she offers you these facts because she can hear in your voice a lingering blame, a conviction that you would have done things differently.

"He would have killed me if I'd stayed," she says, her indignation rising. "And that would have been bad for those kids, too."

You think of your own father's angry, tenor bellows, and the tire squeal at midnight preceding his long, complete silence.

"At least then they wouldn't have blamed you," you say.

"What?" she says.

"Nothing."

MICHELLE IS AT THE DOOR, THUMBS LOOPED into the faded waistband of her jeans. She has a black eye, one cheek swelling dark and red along the bone. She grins at you as you peer through the thick glass pane of the door, still clutching your history textbook by its creaking spine.

"Do you have ten bucks?" she asks, when you open it. "I need to take a taxi to the hospital."

Before you can say anything, she adds, "I'm not taking him back," as though you had asked her. She hugs her arms to her chest, blinks until her eyes begin to look earnest. You get the feeling that you are being lied to.

"I'll see what I have," you say, stepping away from the door. Her manner, her show, is distressing. You wonder if she can tell that you are a little afraid, that you would give her anything to make her go away. She strikes you as having the blunt edge of someone who has realized her power over other people.

"Here you go." You hand her two folded five-dollar bills that you were saving for groceries. She takes them and begins backing away to the door of her own apartment. There is no sound of the baby or anyone else moving around inside.

"Thank you so much," she says, speaking quickly. "You're really helping me out. Just gonna grab my jacket," she says. "I'll pay you back tomorrow for sure."

"Great. Okay," you say, though you are thinking, *Don't bother.* "Good luck."

—

YOUR MOTHER SAYS SHE WENT TO MONTREAL, Toronto, San Francisco.

"I've lived everywhere," she says. "I went everywhere trying to get away from him."

But when pressed for details, she gets flustered, claims she can't remember.

"Oh, I don't know. It was so many years ago. I don't remember streets." She pauses. "I know I went to that market they have there, in Toronto."

"Kensington?"

"Yes, that's it. You see?"

In Montreal, she says, he found her. The woman who lived in the next apartment mentioned a broad, moustached man hanging around their building, chewing gum and reading the same old newspaper at all hours. Your mother was sure it was him. You think she must have wondered about the children, where he left them when he decided to chase her across the country. She might have wanted to call out the window, to ask after Mary's first day at school, Christopher's colic, Annette's awful habit of picking her ears.

She fled Montreal the next morning with only what she could carry in her fringed leather purse, the one that made her seem like a hippie. She said it was just as well she left when she did.

"You know what they were doing then, the separatists? Bombs in mailboxes. I tell you, I couldn't wait to get out of there."

You listen to your mother and realize that this fear has shaped her whole life, flattened it into scattered dull ruts, moulded it up into its erratic peaks of childish glee and obsession. It's like it was with the Dalmatian that was taken away from the family down the street. A cowardly dog with a vicious bite and a flummoxing tendency to howl as it ran in circles around its tiny backyard pen. An animal more or less ruined.

She says she hated San Francisco.

"That place was the worst of all. Too many drugs. That's where I met your father. He was the only person there who wasn't into them."

WHEN YOU LEAVE TO GO TO SCHOOL, there is an envelope outside your door, folded in half and taped together. It is heavy with coins totalling about seven dollars. There is writing scrawled on the outside: *Dear L, Here's you're money. Thanks, M.* You drop it in your purse, noting the silence behind the door of her apartment. No shouting, no television, no Journey blaring on the stereo.

In the mailbox, there is a letter from your mother. She likes writing letters, she says—it gives her something to do. Sometimes on the phone she'll tell you about something that happened but won't go into details.

"I don't want to say anything now," she says. "I mailed you a letter."

Often a letter will come with clippings, articles from *Maclean's* or *The Chronicle Herald* tucked inside. Once there was one about birth control pills causing cancer. Another was about an American soldier killed on leave at a local bar. It has never occurred to you to write back.

The letter in your hand now takes up five sheets, back and front, on the notepaper from Universal Studios which is older than you are. Around the printed colour pictures of sound stages and false fronts of buildings on fire, her perfect cursive fills every available space. It is about the hurricane that brushed up against the coast two weeks ago, scattering the city's old trees.

...I put on my slicker and locked the house. It was like standing under a bucket of water being turned upside down. I guess that's why they say raining buckets. The wind was so strong I could barely walk. I was the only one crazy enough to be out there and I tell you, it was really something!! I wasn't afraid, though it was probably the most dangerous thing I've ever done. I read the next day that the waves hit as high as 20 metres with the storm surge...

You put the letter in your purse, too, next to the envelope from Michelle, and you carry them around in there for a month before you can bring yourself to touch or look at them again.

YOU SMELL LEMON CLEANING PRODUCTS as you turn down your hallway, and you know the neighbours have moved out. Betty, the superintendent, calls a hello to you from the doorway of their bathroom, one hand gloved in yellow rubber waving wetly.

"Hello!" she calls. "Just tidying up in here. Can you believe this mess?" She gestures to the beer bottles she has piled up in buckets near the doorway, then disappears back into the bathroom.

"Have they left?" you ask.

"Looks that way," she says. "I noticed the fellow going out early this morning with a bunch of bags, and when I checked the mail they'd left a note."

Betty has a camera in the lobby that she watches on closed-circuit TV in her bedroom. Channel six. Once she asked you how many boyfriends you had. "You should get them to wear different hats," she said, watching you blush, "so I can tell them apart."

Now you peek into the empty apartment, digging your keys out of your purse. "Well, I hope you can manage to rent it out with no notice," you say, and Betty grunts in agreement.

"Oh, I will," she says. "Don't you worry. It's cheap enough, someone'll take it."

With the silence next door, you can't concentrate. Every thump and creak of the building settling puts you on edge, sets your shoulders jumping in alarm. You print out the balance of your essay, your finished pages, the drone of the printer a welcome swaddle of sound. As the sky darkens, you turn on lights, stacking library books in thematic piles along your desk. You pace the hallway, put water on to boil, rinsing out the teapot and rubbing it dry with the bottom of your cotton T-shirt.

As you shake loose the tea leaves, your thoughts drift to your mother, your father, the beater and the lost children. Everyone you have ever looked for or tried to escape. And when you hear a knock at the door, you are frozen as you go to answer, palm clinging to the doorknob, caught somewhere between longing and dread.

Sandy

"I WAS BORN TO DO THIS," she says.

Her eyes are moist and half-opened, as though the birth in question has only recently come to pass and she was brought forth out there on the street, already grown to a full three hundred pounds, her hair slicked down to her skull with blood on her way out into the world. I bring a blanket to swaddle her, tucking it around her shivering bulk, beneath bare shoulders and thighs swollen with goosebumps like huge pages of flesh covered in a cold Braille. A story to be felt out beneath her red halter top and the leather miniskirt ringing her hips like a blown tire.

"Born to do what?" I say, because she's drunk and maybe hurt and I don't want to jump to any conclusions, don't even want to know which ones I'd come to, for I can sense the shape of them already, and they look too familiar, too easy to be useful. I've read that compassion is different from mere pity, and I believe that to be true, but I'm not sure how it feels to inhabit it, to experience the flush of the feeling and know that its source and its end are untainted, free of complacency or smugness.

"My mother," she says, slurring. "She was a hooker, too." Her fingers rub the grey flannel of the blanket as her hands clench and unclench in time with her breathing.

"Oh, yeah?" I say. I don't want to tell her I'm sorry in case she isn't sorry, though it's hard to imagine why she wouldn't be. I sit down on one of the free floor cushions, wrapping my arms around my knees.

Layla, one of my roommates, twitches her shoulder blades beneath a long, crocheted poncho. She is huddled on her bed, a mattress in the corner of the living room piled high with blankets and massage therapy textbooks.

"That's so interesting," she says, leaning forward to scratch her wrist. Layla talks in nervous spurts, as if her words are talismans warding off the pains and judgments of silence.

"My mother's a psychology professor and my father is a Freudian analyst, if you can believe it. But in the end,

that's what really made me not want to go to university."
She cocks her head and sends tumbling down her back
a mass of dark, greasy curls, the heavy mantle that drags
her delicate face, shadowy and birdlike, into beauty.

She squints at our visitor's flip-flops and painted toenails and says, "I didn't want to turn out like my parents,
you know?" The prostitute nods a little with her eyes
closed, settling in further on her left side. A large rhine-
stone charm on a chain stretched tight around her neck
spells *Sandy*.

"Layla," says Rory, another roommate. She sounds
exasperated. "Be quiet."

Then all we can hear is the sound of Sandy's noisy
breathing, like the wheezing top register of an accordion, her strange arrival inviting speculation like a pebble
courts an oyster.

IT COULD BE THAT SANDY is not really named Sandy.

On the reserve, her name was Alexandra Laughingbrook, but
everybody called her Allie, or sometimes Al, because she had an
uncle named Al who was brazen and good-naturedly foul-mouthed
in a way reminiscent of Sandy's own fits as a toddler, when she
would scream her way in and out of tantrums without sulking or
shedding a single tear.

So they were Big Al and Little Al to the family, even after

Little Al grew up to be bigger than Big Al. He joked that she could fit two of him into the mass around her stomach alone. Then he would say that's how she got so big in the first place: she was a man-eater, like in the song by Hall & Oates. When he saw her striding up to the door of the house he still shared with his parents, he sang, "Watch out, boys, she'll chew you up!" It was the kind of thing that might hurt the feelings of other girls, but Sandy didn't care if people called her fat, because she was. She only got upset if people called her boring, or a goodie-goodie.

It was a doctor who gave her the name Sandy when she was thirteen. Not a real doctor, though he liked to be called that, but a professor, from the university, who was writing a book. He made friends with Sandy right off, even though he was supposed to be there to visit with the elders and record their stories. But Sandy caught his eye one day when she was over at her grandfather's house, berating the old man for wearing an ugly sweater.

"Granddad, you're a good-looking guy," she said. "But no one will want to kiss you if you look like a dirty sheepdog."

"That must be why Nana bought it for me," he said, and Sandy giggled and rubbed her soft hands up and down the hairy sleeves of the sweater. The professor asked Sandy what she thought of his own sweater, which was a thick, cable-knit cardigan with brown leather elbow patches, and she told him that it was a nice enough sweater for an egghead.

Every time she insulted the professor he practically clapped his hands together in glee. He said he was thinking of changing his research focus. Young people on the reservation had a kind of unspoiled crudeness, he said. They were as hyper and hormonal as teenagers in the city, but without the repressiveness or confused fear. Everything was carried out in a kind of innocence. Grand-dad told the professor he ought to watch out because he seemed to be in danger of thinking he was the first person to think his own thoughts, but Sandy liked the way that he seemed to adore her and was always at her ear, goading her on.

He began calling her Sandy because he said it was a pretty name that was also an adjective, one that could transform her name into a description, into a beautiful part of the landscape.

"It's like the banks of the creek that runs alongside the bound-ary road," he said, his glasses gleaming in the light, "at the end of a long summer, when the water is down to a trickle but still lively. Sandy Laughingbrook, that's you, you see? You're part of this place."

"You're retarded," said Sandy, spitting out her gum onto the ground. "Just totally fucked." But her tone implied a grudging admiration.

RORY PUTTERS IN THE KITCHEN, still wearing her down jacket, with the brusqueness of acknowledged guilt. She is the one who invited Sandy to our apartment during a drunken encounter on our street the night before. Caleb and Stuart, two of our other roommates, found Sandy asleep on the doorstep and called Rory at the restaurant. There was a long pause before Rory admitted that she'd had a conversation with her in the early hours of the morning.

"She was crying," said Rory, "and bleeding, and delirious. And I was totally wasted and I didn't know how to help." Rory said she might have pointed toward our apartment. "I think I told her she could come to me for help if she ever got into trouble."

IN THE OLD DAYS, Sandy liked courting trouble.

Sandy used to be very big into sound effects. She would make a sound like a phone hanging up in someone's ear: "Click, uhhhhnnnnnn." She used it as a kind of retort when she was annoyed with someone. Big Al would tell her to do the dishes and she would say, "Sorry, I'm busy! Click, uhhhhnnnnnn." When the professor said, "Take your shirt off," she said, "You're a pervert. Click, uhhhhnnnnnn." But sometimes she would take it off anyway.

It was the professor who gave her the necklace, with "Sandy" spelled out in a glittering stones. He'd had it made to order in the city. The necklace was a gift but also a bribe to keep quiet. But it's not like Sandy wanted anyone to know. She shoved the necklace into a drawer, which she emptied into a box years later when she moved away. She only took to wearing it when she started working for Jimmy because he said Alexandra was too fancy a name for an escort as big as she was.

"Not that I'm saying there aren't guys who are into fatties," he said. "But nobody wants a girl who thinks too much of herself."

NOW RORY IS LOOKING ODD in her unease. Her hands keep flying to her black headband, pushing it up and back on her forehead until it begins to show traces of kitchen debris, faint fingermarks in flour and cigarette ash.

"It's not your fault," says Rory, and Sandy's eyelids flutter. It is impossible to tell whether she's listening or what Rory might mean. A counter with peeling laminate divides the kitchen from the living room, and Caleb is perched on it in an awkward pose, his grubby wool sweater rubbing up against the dish rack. One of his feet, idly kicking, hits Rory's elbow, and she slaps his shin with more irritation than playfulness.

"Get down from there," she says.

"Some anarchist you are," says Caleb. He slips off and remains standing in the corner, arms crossed. Stuart is fiddling with the buttons on the military jacket that makes him look like a *Nutcracker* extra, his eyes moving from face to face.

Rory fixes on Sandy as she whips the teabags in and out of the pot, her chapped lips parted in an expression of swollen sympathy. "It's not your fault," she repeats louder, as this time Sandy nods, lifting a hand toward her cheek as if to scratch it, but instead only bumping her chin with her wristwatch.

"Ow. Yeah, I know," she says, and coughs in what might be meant for a laugh. "Family business." She fully opens her left eye and peers with it in Rory's direction, though she is not at the right angle to see her. She adds, "Though it was a bit of the drugs, too." Her brown eye sliding shut gives the impression of a wink and Caleb lets loose a hoot of nervous laughter.

"I mean, isn't it always," he mutters as Rory glares.

SANDY'S SIZE may be deceptive.

Like a boulder on the side of a mountain, she looks as solid and heavy as if she could rest without stirring for a thousand years, her size belying a vast potentiality of movement, the extra flesh on her frame concealing the muscle beneath. She once used her elbow to connect with the jaw of a man who butted out a cigarette on her leg, who clutched at the back of her white rayon shirt as she forced her way out of the car. He shouted through a mouthful of blood, sputtering threats, but Sandy slammed the door in his face with a heave of her hip.

Being big, it takes a lot of booze to get her drunk, so she doesn't knock back often, or at least not on her own tab. She used to drink a lot at first, but now she's cutting down. She says she's never wasted, but always buzzed.

RORY'S HANDS ARE SHAKY as she pours the tea, spilling some into the sink.

"Fuck," she says. Having granted the prostitute her strange absolution, she seems jumpy. "Who wants tea?" she asks, and everyone says yes except Sandy. Rory brings her the first cup in one of Stuart's prized recycled mugs, one with a cartoon of a guy on a toilet with the caption, *Coffee really gets you going!!* Anything we find in the garbage we call recycled: coffee mugs, bookshelves, bananas. Dumpster diving is Stuart's main form of contribution to the apartment, as he claims it is the best way out of becoming a wage slave. He says once you know where to look, you'll find that people will throw away almost anything.

"Here you go," says Rory, crouching at Sandy's side. She holds the cup of green tea level with Sandy's midriff, which is spilling out from between her top and skirt like bread dough beginning to rise. "Drink this."

"Uhn," says Sandy. "What is it?"

"Tea."

"Oh, no thanks. I mean, thanks very much. I just

want to thank you all so much for all your help. Thanks so much. Thanks for just letting me sit here." Her eyes slide closed again as she speaks.

Rory looks at me, and Caleb and Stuart look embarrassed, each casting down his eyes to some non-essential task, feigning absorption—Caleb rearranging items in the cutlery drawer as Stuart peels off the tiny 9/11 headlines that someone once pasted onto our airplane-shaped telephone. Layla stretches out for the tea from her spot on the mattress and splashes a little on a blanket as she settles back down. She frowns.

"Is anyone doing laundry later?" she asks, dabbing at the spot with another corner of the blanket, though she is usually the first one to finally crack and lug her clothes in garbage bags to the laundromat on the corner.

Rory grabs me by the wrist and pulls me to my feet.

"Come on, Allie. We'll go see how much we have," she says, pulling me down the hall.

SANDY MIGHT BE A STICKLER for clean clothes.

She once repaired a washing machine by herself, tracing the source of the leak with a page of the Pennysaver classifieds. Slipped under during the delicate cycle, the newsprint mapped the drip. With her plump hands, she took the machine apart and felt it all over, exploring every crevice, feeling for spring catches, chipping the polish

*on her long fingernails into Rorschach tests of dark red blotches.
Friends said she did it as though by instinct, like a thrush turning
tail to South America, or a baby that seeks the breast even as it
learns to breathe. Sandy figured out how the thing was put together,
and with a screwdriver borrowed from the girl next door, flipped
back the control panel, unhooked the wiring, and hauled off the
cabinet, laying it in her dingy shower. When she found the hole, she
mended it with a Phillips-head screw and a piece of gum.*

*For Sandy, the washer is a mark of pride. It came with the
apartment and she knows her landlord will never pay to have it
fixed. On Wednesday nights most of Jimmy's girls come over and
wash their underwear and paint each other's nails. They pay Sandy
in mickeys of vodka which they help her drink.*

IN THE BATHROOM, RORY TWISTS HER BROWN HAIR around
her knuckles until her fingertips turn dark and blood-
logged. The rank smell of the tub wafts up beside us as
we perch along its wide, chipped rim. There's no one on
earth who could keep this bathroom clean with the five of
us living here in what is really a one-bedroom flophouse,
and so nobody really tries. Layla is the only one who will
drag the soap-scummed hair from the drain when the water starts to pool, stagnating in grey puddles in the shower.
We keep our shoes on inside because of the mess, and
because the landlord, René, pulled up the carpet when we

moved in but never came back to take away the tack strips. They still line every edge of the apartment, deterrents to wallflowers and the barefoot.

"We've got to get rid of her," whispers Rory. "I completely realize that."

Her face is sober and strange, neither her drinking nor her game face. She is worrying her striped knit gloves, pulling them on and off in turn, and I can see the red patch of scar on her palm from where a tear gas canister exploded in her hand in Quebec City. She was throwing them back over the fence at the police, screaming obscenities and pacifist slogans in turn.

There is no trace of that fierceness now, of that tough yet pliable conviction. There is just a limpness to her expression as though her face has lost its elasticity, like the burned skin on her hand that is slowly gnarling her fingers into a clenched grip.

"It's not that she's a prostitute," I say at last. "Right? It's just that we all have things to do and it wouldn't be safe to leave her alone here."

I feel the shadow of Rory's usual self-righteousness hovering around us, a hungry ghost. Though it drifts from her, it is still present, and judging.

Rory nods. "It's not that we can't trust her," she says. "But people in her situation are sometimes driven to do things they wouldn't otherwise consider." She looks at the shower curtain, hanging lopsidedly off two plastic rings. "I know I don't have any material possessions of note, but I'd still be pissed if they were stolen. And you have your books."

"Yes," I say. "That's true." I picture strangers in our apartment, running their hands along the dusty shelves, under the stale sheets, looking for valuables. "Though I doubt they'd fetch a good price on the black market."

Rory's hushed laugh comes out with a snort. "Let's go." She sighs as she stands. "At least if her pimp showed up he'd probably take her away."

MAYBE SANDY AND HER PIMP planned the whole thing.

Jimmy had seen those kids sitting on the roof, getting high, watching the girls get in and out of cars all night. They made him nervous. It was impossible to tell what they might do. Their house might be full of drugs, but they were from money, most of them. University people. Uptight about sex. Jimmy told Sandy that she should hit them up for some cash some time.

"What, a sob story?" she said. She was doing her makeup, gold and burnt-sienna eyes. Sandy was never hesitant with the colour. Not needing to hold back was one of the few perks of being a hooker.

"Sure," said Jimmy. "Or you know what, maybe me and

*Andy'll just go in there some night when we know they're out.
They've probably got some stereos. And weed."*

"Yeah."

*Sandy was self-conscious when she saw the people who lived in
the apartment above the hair salon. She liked the way they wore
their clothes, the way they were always gathered together in a big
group. It reminded her of how she used to be with her cousins.*

*One night she saw them splitting a joint, its burning end an
orange star moving between the shadowed figures on the shingles.
She saw the glint of a toe ring on Layla's bare foot, a beer bottle in
Caleb's left hand.*

*"Right on," she said aloud. She raised her arm and waved,
but nobody noticed except a passing car, which slowed down at the
corner ahead to let her in.*

THERE IS A THUDDING ON THE FRONT DOOR as we move
back to the living room, then a kind of timid scrabbling.
I look to Rory, wondering whether a pimp could really
burst in on us like a *deus ex machina*, wild in a possessive
rage. But Rory is only looking at Sandy, her green eyes
fixed minty bright and blank upon the prostitute's face.

Caleb answers the door, and it is a woman with a clipboard, dark brushed hair, and a tailored wool coat. She
looks cold, and a bit doubtful about the elevated porch,
which René began hacking down in one of his optimistic

renovation phases. He abandoned the new porch project just inches away from having sawn through the first of the support pillars. Since then, the porch has leaned noticeably to the west, listing like a ship in a storm.

Stuart whispers *Narc* before the woman at the door asks to speak to the person in charge.

"In charge of what?" I ask, at the same time as Rory says, "No one's in charge."

"Of whatever it is you've got going on here," says the woman, raising her eyebrows. "I'm Linda Naylor, from the Salvation Army down the street." She nods her head to the right, then shakes it, pointing left. "That way, actually. Anyway, we heard that there was a new safe house being set up here, and it's our policy to carry out an inspection before we begin making referrals."

"Who told you we were a safe house?" asks Layla from her corner.

Linda consults her clipboard. "It was reported to us by a sex worker this morning. A woman named Kylie. She said her friend was staying here."

She waits for a response, and I watch her face as she takes in the orange sponge-painted walls, the multiple mattresses, the beer bottles stacked up along the counter. "I can tell you you're going to need to put in a lot of work here if you hope to run a viable shelter," she says. "And you'll need the landlord's approval, as well."

"This is crazy," says Caleb, scratching his beard. "We're not a shelter." He looks to Stuart, who is loitering behind the open door, ready to slam it shut, if necessary.

"Word travels fast, I guess," says Stuart, and shrugs.

Shooting Stuart a stern glance, Linda says, "I hope you guys haven't been trying to rent rooms out by the hour like that place down the street."

"What? No," I say. "We're not trying to do anything. Is that why you're here?"

Linda looks past me, over at Sandy, whose breathing has regulated into the rhythms of deep sleep, although whether from exhaustion or artifice I can't tell. I thought I'd noticed her tilting farther over on her side, angling her face away from the door, as Caleb reached to open it.

"Is that Ceci?" asks Linda. I shake my head no.

"Her necklace says Sandy," I say.

Linda nods. "That's her." The back of her metal clipboard glints in the light from the star-shaped lamp overhead as she folds it to her chest, chin tilted up in Rory's direction. "Hi, Ceci," she calls. "It's Linda. Are you okay?"

Sandy makes no response. I can only blink at her real name, wondering at my own surprise.

"So what is she doing here?" asks Linda in a lowered voice.

Rory steps forward and says, "I invited her. She said she wanted some place to lie down."

Linda peers first at Rory, then at Sandy, watching the soft rise and fall of her chest. "Okay, fine. Do you want me to call someone?" she asks. "The police have a holding cell she could dry out in."

"We'll take care of it," I say, and Stuart adds, "No thanks. Goodbye." He pushes the door shut and we listen as Linda's footsteps echo as she slowly descends one stair at a time.

SANDY MIGHT BE THE PROSTITUTE who mouthed off to my mother one night a few years ago. My mother was waiting for the bus to her evening shift at the hospital.

"Hey lady," said Sandy. "You're on my corner." It was a corner just two blocks down from our own dilapidated apartment, on the same bleak stretch of urban road, unknown to pedestrians other than those who lived directly along it.

My mother, in her late fifties and wearing a blue down coat like a queen-sized bedspread, just pointed at the sign. She was a stout woman who liked seeing people who were even more overweight than she was. She enjoyed any occasion for verbal sparring. "This is a bus stop," she said. There would have been a satisfied belligerence in her voice.

Sandy just raised one shoulder. Her arms were wrapped around her body, hands stuffed into the warmth of her armpits. "That doesn't change the fact that it's my corner." She too wore a dowdy winter coat, but her bare legs were visible below the hem, thick and bluish in the cold above grey sneakers. She was shifting from side to side in a shivering dance. It was late February.

"Well, what do you suggest I do?" my mother demanded, and her grey curls quivered. "I'm not moving until the bus comes. And I'm not walking down to the next stop. I have arthritis, I'll have you know." She tightened her grip on her purse strap, gesturing down at her massive coat. "Are you afraid I'm going to cut into your business?" She sniffed. "Are your customers all blind or something?"

Sandy's lip curled and her voice became a pitchy shout, her shrieks blown hollow with the wind: "Look, lady, all I'm saying is you don't want to mess with me. I know people."

"I'll bet you do," said my mother. She pointed across the street with one large yellow mitten. "Why don't you just go wait over there until the bus comes? You can do what you want—I'm not moving."

But she never found out what Sandy would have done because just then a car pulled over on the other side of the street and Sandy ran over, her laces skimming the asphalt. "I better not see you here when I get back," she called over her shoulder, and laughed. Smiling, her face looked childish, her huge cheeks dimpling up round and merry.

My mother was tickled. It was one of her favourite stories, when the prostitute told her off and she sassed right back.

WHEN SANDY OPENS HER EYES, the room shrinks. She is alert now, and watchful, her personality burgeoning large and fearsome. My stories slide off her, fall down her broad back onto the floor, like the blanket now heaping at her feet as she struggles up, muttering curses and incomprehensible phrases. I feel a sense of betrayal in the discontinuity, a deflation.

"Better be going," she says at last. There is a coherent element in her voice now, an aspect in her manner that suggests a nose for trouble and for avoiding it. I wonder if she thinks we might call the police on her after all. Her hands travel to the waistband of her skirt, smoothing it down over the top of her thighs. "Sorry to have started any trouble for you folks," she says.

She lumbers to the door, almost tripping over another floor cushion, grabbing onto Stuart's offered elbow.

"See ya," she says, and with a shove of her huge forearm against the door, she slips outside, back into the cold.

SANDY MIGHT NOT REMEMBER this.

Sandy lies to social workers all the time. She'll tell them any-

thing if they'll give her a break, if they don't make it obvious she's just another lost cause. She wavers between deploring that nobody cares and scoffing at the naïveté of the people who try to help. Sometimes their optimism or their pity is infectious; other times she mimics them to Jimmy, as a joke.

Sometimes, when she loses her footing, she stumbles with the weight of the hope people have heaped on her, like when she ridiculed the man who wanted her to sing to him afterward, a lullaby, as a mother might. She saw his fury rise as she laughed, then laughed harder when her cheek stung with a slap. Sometimes she drinks and, if she can be bothered, she forgets. It is tiring, carrying other people's shame all day and all night like some beast of burden. Like sex itself, fraught and disgraced.

Like anyone, she fights the pull between facelessness and notoriety, between meaningfulness and death. She tries to let people think what they want, and for the most part she doesn't care. Sometimes she helps her friends with a little perspective, with a cheeky quip on how they're better off, on how they can see through the bland existence of other people and the emptiness at its core. Other times she is amazed at the way a woman can move through space and time and it is just called a life. As though it were nothing more remarkable than that.

The Republic of Rose Island

DANIEL LIKES TO TELL THE STORY of how we met, an edited version that leaves out everything to do with Lisa. He leaves out a lot, because mostly it had nothing to do with him at all.

Georgie phoned in a robbery, he says, and guess who got sent.

Daniel is a cop who showers daily, maintains a well-stocked bird feeder in the winter, and volunteers with Big Brothers. He spends time worrying about at-risk youth.

I tell him that not all children of single parents turn out screwed up. Lisa and I were raised by our widowed father, a dealer in rare coins and stamps. He maintained a cramped shop well known to collectors across the country and stored all his goods in special protective cases resistant to heat, light, and pipe-tobacco smoke. He died of emphysema when we were in our late twenties.

I didn't have a Big Sister, I said, and I turned out okay.

Well, you did have a big sister, he said. Lisa. Someone to keep you company when your dad wasn't home.

Lisa was only technically a big sister, at fourteen months older than me, with strong tendencies, as I saw them when we were teenagers, toward flightiness and immaturity. I dubbed her Most Likely to Let Everybody Down. Only because she was affectionate but forgetful and I adored her. She would do things like promise to French braid my hair before picture day and then leave early while I was in the shower.

Daniel said, but you had someone else you could talk to. So maybe that's what made the difference.

IT WAS A SLOW DAY, AS DANIEL TELLS IT, so they dispatched someone over right away. They always send a rookie out on calls like that.

When Daniel came to the door of my tiny house, I was pacing the hallway between the kitchen and the living room, rubbing my upper arms with my hands, sweat drizzling my eyebrows.

I showed him the scene of the crime: my back door and the area of the small, carpeted living room immediately to its left. I haven't touched anything, I said.

Are you all right, ma'am? he asked. He was looking at me strangely. I stared until he touched the top of his forehead, nodding toward me. My goggles, still strapped with their elastic to the back of my head but pushed up to rest along my hairline. I pulled them off.

It's for my work, I said. Cutting glass, stained glass.

It had started out as a hobby and had turned into almost a living. My bread and butter was making lampshades with patterns of different animals running. Bunnies leaping, monkeys gambolling. They were selling in six different stores downtown, where rich people bought them, I was told, to put in their children's bedrooms. My specialty was cutesy stuff, whimsy, sometimes a little rock and roll, like the KISS window hanging I'd made for one customer. Not just your usual floral patterns, anyway. Some made-to-order stuff. More and more now.

Daniel had pen and paper out. So walk me through it, he said. You came home and noticed someone had broken in through the back door.

I shook my head. I was home the whole time, I said.

So you were home at the time of the burglary?

That's right.

But you didn't notice anything?

Maybe. I don't know. I had the electric grinder on down in the basement, and it's a bit noisy. I did become uneasy at some point and decided to come upstairs. Maybe I heard a strange footstep but didn't register it.

Telling the story released some of the pressure in my chest. I took in Daniel's strong jaw as I exhaled. His serene blue eyes.

And that's when you noticed that someone had broken in?

Well, no. Not right away. I leave the screen door un-latched, sometimes, in the hot weather. I just forget to lock it, I guess. But that doesn't mean I'm inviting people in.

Every minute I felt more soothed, talking to this tow-headed officer. Even in his first year on the force, Daniel looked trustworthy, efficient. I guessed he was a few years younger than me. I had the hopeful but bizarre thought that his youth would mean he'd want to prove himself, make good on my case.

I said, it was when I saw that the milk crate was gone that I realized someone had been here. It was full of old Archie comics. I pointed to the corner, beside the big jade plant. That's where I kept it, normally. You can see its imprint on the rug.

A block of crisscrossed indentations stamped the spot, and Daniel looked at it for a moment, his brow furrowing.

And nothing else was taken?

I shook my head. No, not that I can tell.

So while you were at home with your door unlocked, someone came in and stole your Archie comic collection?

I nodded. Yes.

Was this a valuable collection, ma'am?

Well, honestly, I don't know. It's my sister's. But I doubt it. Not terribly so, anyways. Only dating back to the seventies.

And then he laughed. Can I ask why you decided to call this in?

His eyes were warm, but I blinked, gaped, as my pulse started up again, the pounding in my ears from when I discovered the crate missing. It's a crime, isn't it? I asked him. Prowling around somebody's house and taking their stuff? How would you like it?

Daniel tucked his pad of paper away in a breast pocket.

I'm sorry, he said. I wouldn't, you're right. But you know what? I think it was probably just a kid. I don't think you need to worry about being safe in here.

I burst into tears. I might even have still been talking, I don't remember, but I was given over in a matter of seconds to raggedy, gasping sobs, my arms crossed over my chest.

Daniel made an awkward exit, leaving his card on the counter.

"Don't worry, ma'am, I will be writing this up. Don't you worry."

Daniel likes to dwell on this part, evoking me at my frailest. Though to keep things light, he colours it as a kind of mild hysteria, flipping it into comic relief, a justified outrage at the indifference of the police. He is good at telling this story. He makes it very believable.

Georgie started screaming at me about her tax dollars, he says. Asking where I got off determining the relative value of things. Stuff about my badge number and having me written up. He winks sometimes and says, taking sensitivity training was also something that she suggested to me. But I was pretty much sold on that by the time I got out of there, anyway.

THE NEXT DAY I RAN INTO HIM, out of uniform, at the grocery store. He was wearing a white buttoned shirt and brown dress shoes that seemed newish. He was ahead of me at the checkout, buying spaghetti sauce and Cheerios.

When he saw me, his eyes lit up and he plucked something out of the magazine rack, holding it to his chest.

Afternoon, he said. He looked both earnest and a little amused. Maybe I can start making amends to you and your sister, he said. He offered me the comic book he'd just grabbed. It was a *Little Archie*, a new one.

Oh geez, I said, blowing my nose. I took it from him. These ones are really terrible. I flipped it open. Miniature versions of the characters, caught up in the same rivalries and passions they would re-enact as teenagers, ad nauseum. A pretty pessimistic take on personal growth. Lisa's enthusiasm for the comic had always seemed strange, though she claimed to get a kick out of its old-fashioned worldview—where the worst thing that could happen to you was showing up at the sock hop in the same dress as somebody else.

I'm sorry I upset you yesterday, Daniel said, noting my red-rimmed eyes. I hope I can convince you to forgive me.

It's not you, I said. I'm not normally a basketcase. It's my sister. She's gone missing.

He wouldn't bother telling this story, risk distressing me by bringing it up, except that people always ask. When you've got two people like me and Daniel, what we do and what we're like, people always want to know how we got together. And though Daniel can stretch the truth for what he thinks is a higher purpose, he's a terrible liar in general. So he sticks to the facts, more or less.

When he tells it, though, the box full of comics is mine.

→

THE STRANGEST THING TO MY FATHER about Lisa's collection was its incompleteness. He offered to take her to comic book conventions, but she never wanted to go. She just bought the odd issue at the grocery store that she read and reread and refused to part with. This was difficult for my father to understand, for it was his skill in collecting, above any of his other talents, by which he had supported himself for most of his adult life.

He owned his shop outright. *Wright & Sons, Philately and Numismatics,* scrolled in modest italics across the letterhead. It was stodgy-sounding, even as *Wright & Fils, philatélie et numismatique,* as it appeared in faded letters on the shop's outside sign. He named it before we were born, before he was even married. He bought it from a button guy who was moving across the Plateau to a bigger location, so the place had a long history in the vending of tiny objects, the cracks in the floorboards always rooted out and patched in a hurry. For my father, the coin aspect was only a sideline, though he sometimes sold a cheap variety bag of world currency to a kid just starting out a collection. It was the stamps that were his obsession.

He'd been started on collecting by his own father, and what with that and the name of the store, there was no doubt a dynasty was on his mind. But though he brought us there as children every Saturday morning, Lisa and I never caught the bug. It could have been something to do with the rules: the coins were too dirty for us to touch, and we were too dirty to touch the stamps. The oil of our skin was liable to cause damage, so our father instructed us in the tedious use of his special rubber-tipped tongs, hovering over us with an apprehensive eye. As a result, we usually ended up killing time by flipping through the catalogues, Stanley Gibbons's *Stamps of the World* and the Darnell *Stamps of Canada*, memorizing and calling out the names of the rarest ones on the off chance we should stumble upon one slapped onto an old envelope. This only until we were old enough to object to going at all.

My father sold most of the valuable stamps that passed through his hands but maintained his own modest collection. He had six beautiful 1929 Bluenoses mounted in a frame with a deep blue matte, as well as three decent examples of Brazil's famous 1843 bull's eyes—only the second set of world stamps ever issued. He pointed them out to every new customer who walked in.

But in general he tended to favour the intricately designed as well as the roundly obscure. His favourite stamps were mint sheets from an Italian micronation. Named the Republic of Rose Island, it had been erected upon a large platform off the coast of Rimini by an engineer in 1968. The stamps were a souvenir for the tourists, as well as a sly display of sovereignty, and the Italian government reacted by seizing control and destroying the whole structure by dynamite within less than a year. Each sheet of stamps bore an image documenting a stage of Rose Island's history: its creation, its occupation, and its rapid obliteration.

It's something grandiose, said my father, offering up his wooden-handled magnifying glass, making up your own country out of concrete and stamps. He had a longstanding admiration for Giorgio Rosa, the inventor, founder, and president of Rose Island.

It's something egomaniacal, you mean, said Lisa. She took the proffered glass and pretended to be unimpressed, peering through at the tricolour stamps and at the white shield with three clustered roses that decorated the top of the selvage. She liked to tease him, but I felt closest to my father at these times, when he gave himself over to this kind of fancy, this fondness.

LISA HAD VERY FEW POSSESSIONS OF VALUE. Everything good had been bought during a nesting period, when some variety of handsome man holed up with her in her apartment, letting her bring home pizzas for supper, readily agreeing to her fair-minded divvying up of the bills according to income. Since she worked as a social worker and community organizer, she met a lot of students, a lot of volunteers and passionate advocates of various causes, whose fervour translated into the ability to fall wildly and wisely in love with her.

The nice things she purchased tended to leak away in the separation stage—where, by indifference or despair or a sheer eagerness to be free, she let the things fall away from her as easily as the men themselves, ending up lighter by half than when she came in. She'd suffer losses in material possessions and in her fighting spirit for true love—though since she had more than her fair share of the spirit, she lived to love again without much difficulty or even a waiting period. Her only overriding concern was that time was running out for her to have a baby.

I hate that I'm a fucking cliché, she said, but the

clock is ticking.

Sometimes she moved out, though more often they did, lugging a yellow couch or a set of white lamps out the door with them. The problem, Lisa said, is that I always let them choose the colour. All I do is pay.

I was always reproachful of this leniency, and sour on the men who professed a robust anti-materialism upon moving in yet managed to seem bereft during the breakup.

I gave Tim some pillows and forks and knives and stuff, said Lisa, once we'd decided to call it quits. The coffee mugs and the futon. Oh, and the small desk. He needs some things just to live. He has nothing.

You don't want to split up a set of cutlery, I lamented, but Lisa only shrugged.

But I wasn't really entitled to blame her, since I only did the opposite, letting lovers in and then drawing their things to myself, the refuse, the trifles they couldn't be bothered to make away with when they left. Over the years I had accumulated a few of my own trophies and mementos. Old sleeping bags. Wool sweaters. Paperbacks already read and discarded, like *Zorba the Greek* and *Slaughterhouse-Five*. But nothing new in a long time.

So although I had established a diverse, livable clutter at the time of the robbery, I had none of the things that normally fall prey to robbers. No jewellery, no computer, no stereo. The extent of my electronics was a wonky clock radio in the bedroom which persisted in embellishing every hour with the number eight, no matter what the time (81:24, 82:06, 87:39). It had the virtue of a being a faultless receiver, picking up every station in reach with nearly perfect fidelity, but that could never be guessed by a thief. There were sheets of coloured glass in the basement, and other valuable supplies for my work, but nothing obvious or easy to make off with. So when I saw that the crate was missing, at first I thought it was a mistake.

Lisa had brought over the milk crate a few months before she went missing, citing artistic differences with a promising new man she was seeing. An executive. She said she had two words to describe the relationship: exhilarating and fraught. She said, I've never had such great sex in my life. Though I can't tell if it's him or just turning thirty-five that's done it. Sexual peak and all that.

I tried to skim past what could turn into talk of her orgasms. Why fraught? I asked.

Because there's another woman.

Not again, I said.

It's not like that. Lisa's face fairly bloomed with earnestness. We're all friends. We're open. It's called polyamory. He's actually very progressive, socially, for someone so enmeshed in capitalism by his work. We're all free to take as many lovers as we want. In this case, he's seeing both of us.

Very Betty and Veronica of you, I said.

Very, she agreed. But it's best if I keep these over here. His aesthetic sensibility is a little different from mine. All black and white and smooth, blank surfaces. Anti-kitsch.

I didn't ask why she couldn't have just pushed them to the back of one of her own closets, piled the top of the crate with dirty clothes. I already knew that Lisa didn't like doing things by half once she had made up her mind.

Fine, I said. Just put them somewhere out of the way.

She plopped them down just behind where she was standing, in the corner of the living room, probably so she wouldn't have to take her shoes off, a rule I had that was a sore point between us.

THE MAN IN QUESTION was Will McDaid. Lisa said he was one of the Black Irish, which I supposed meant he didn't have red hair. Before long, I gathered that he was beautiful and cruel, or at the very least careless with Lisa's feelings. He had a number of other significant virtues (intelligence, wealth, and charm) to offer as compensation, or so claimed my sister, who was besotted in a way I had never before witnessed.

Unlike other boyfriends, who alighted on the surface of her life only to float away later, Will had burrowed his way in like a tick, producing a persistent itch and wielding an influence over every aspect of her life, though whether it was by his design or hers, I couldn't tell. One day after I'd tipped half a latte down my chest at the café, I was poking around in her closet and complimented her on some new outfits I saw hanging— sleek, well-cut blazers and pants, fitted dresses, tasteful in beige and charcoal—and she told me Will had helped her pick them out.

They're great, I said. He has an eye. But does he know where you work?

The centre where Lisa worked hosted everyone from church groups to labour unionists and drug addicts. I'd visited, and the dress code was fiercely casual. The closest thing I'd seen to a dress shirt was plaid flannel. Lisa herself mostly wore jeans.

Won't it alienate your clientele? I asked. She was frowning.

She said, I'll look more put together and that in turn

will inspire confidence.

All right, I said. Sure.

Lisa also hinted that she had begun waxing, everywhere. This was not her usual habit.

I'm getting a rash from it, she said.

I winced. Ouch, I said. But I was oddly fascinated. Previously, Lisa's biggest nod to personal grooming was buying a pair of nail clippers, as she used to maintain the length of her toenails by biting, the same method she used on her hands. She had the flexibility of a yogi and was fond of sitting folded up like a pipe cleaner, knees by her shoulders, like a chick scrunched into an egg. Once I saw her inspect her foot and bring it idly toward her mouth as we watched a movie.

If anyone else ever caught you doing that, I told her, you would never hear the end of it.

There were other changes. Lisa's calls, which had always been regular but spaced out—she preferred dropping by to talking on the phone—became frequent and urgent, clustered in needy bursts followed by long intervals of silence during which, for my own peace of mind, I presumed her to be happy. These conversations were mostly spent analyzing her relationship, sifting for meaning through the detritus of Will's constant slights and neglect.

He said he'd call on Monday, she said, but then I didn't hear from him until Friday, when he picked me up after work and took me to Chez Christophe.

Chez Christophe was a very nice restaurant just a couple of blocks away from Will's apartment and our father's old store. Every year after Lisa turned sixteen, our father took us there on our birthdays, indulging in foie gras and sharing a bottle of wine with us, the only two times we'd see him drink throughout the year.

I don't know if the restaurant means anything, I said. He's rich, right? It's just a nice gesture after spending Monday through Thursday with Holly.

We don't know that's what he was doing, said Lisa, sounding disagreeable. He's a busy guy.

MY FATHER'S TEETOTALLING wasn't the only old-fashioned thing about him. There was the pipe, the suspenders, the pressed white handkerchiefs. He also did most of his business by post. Being a stamp dealer, he understood that his customers liked sending and receiving mail, as he did. When we were children, our father encouraged us to solicit penpals from among the children of his customers. Some obliged, and Lisa and I exchanged badly printed missives with children in places like Scotland, Jamaica, and Tennessee, detailing the most superficial aspects of our lives, or occasionally the most vital and secret. *My name is Georgia, but people call me Georgie, and I am eleven years old and in Grade Five. I have brown hair and hazel eyes and one older sister named Lisa. My favourite colour is purple, and I am madly in love with a boy named Aubrey. He has long hair so when we have supply teachers, they always think he is a girl named Audrey. I am hoping that he will notice that I never laugh at that. My favourite animal is the manatee, which people used to think were mermaids. They are endangered because of boats. What is your favourite animal? Do you like your school? Please write back soon.*

These correspondences petered out after the usual fashion, but something about the minutiae of those letters, which I still have in a box somewhere, managed to convey a small part of my father's wonder for objects, their ability to evoke a particular time and place. The process also cultivated in me an affection for letter-writing. My most successful relationships tended to be the long-distance ones, where I struck up a romance with someone just about due to leave town.

In spite of my comparative inexperience in love, Lisa still hailed me as her prime consultant. After some time had passed in her relationship, Lisa's calls of misery developed into planning sessions to strategize how Will might best be convinced to drop Holly and date only her.

Isn't that counter to the spirit of your agreement? I asked. Your free-love compact?

There was a pause as though I'd hit a nerve. Lisa was extremely susceptible to guilt. It was why she made such a good activist.

But a month or so later, when Will and Holly stopped seeing each other for undisclosed reasons, nothing seemed to improve. Lisa was almost beside herself.

Do you think he's met somebody new? she asked, after a week went by, the hoarseness of her voice hinting at prolonged crying, or possibly cigarettes, her guilty solace. I mean, somebody else? He's still impossible to get a hold of. She sounded baffled.

He's just a dog, I told her. Isn't it obvious?

I GOT IMPATIENT WITH THE WHOLE THING. The next time Lisa stopped by it was in the early morning while I was scoring a virgin piece of opalescent buttercup glass, pushing the cutter forward in a smooth arc. I heard the doorbell, which I ignored, and then Lisa's telltale assured thumping. I came to the door determined to be disgruntled, having cracked the design piece as I'd tried to separate it.

I thought you could make me breakfast, Lisa said, face wan. Least you could do for your favourite sister.

She stepped inside and shrugged out of her khaki trenchcoat. She was altogether more carefully groomed than I'd seen her this side of high school, with glossed lips and dark eye makeup, though that was already smudging. She'd had her hair cut in a salon instead via of her usual DIY method in her bathroom at home: it hung straight and smooth with a fashionable, thick bang. She looked beautiful and exhausted.

Leave your shoes on if you like, I said, leading the way to the kitchen. She sat at the tiny wooden table as I put on the coffee.

I think I'm ending it, she said at length.

Really?

Don't look so thrilled, she said. I shrugged, pressing my lips together as my eyebrows waggled, and she laughed.

I'm just a wreck, she said. I'm not cut out for this whole non-monogamy thing.

Of course not, I said. Who is? I sliced a bagel and popped it into the toaster.

I didn't hear from her for three days after that and then spotted her on a patio on St. Denis, picking at a plate of vegetarian nachos, sitting with a petite blonde I didn't recognize.

Georgie, said Lisa. My favourite sister. This is Holly.

Holly, this is Georgia.

Holly stretched out a tiny, well-manicured hand, and I shook it, feeling traitorous, realizing I hadn't actually believed them to be friends. Both she and Lisa had broken off their conversation as I'd approached the table, and I caught Holly's eyes darting back to Lisa as our hands dropped back.

Sorry to interrupt, I began, but Holly stood up, shaking her head.

I've actually got to go, she said. She smiled at me. Why don't you take my seat?

I sat, watching as Holly and Lisa kissed goodbye.

Lisa said, I'll be thinking of you.

Thanks, said Holly. I'll see you when you get back.

Where are you going? I asked, once Holly had gone.

Lisa shrugged. Away.

IT WAS EASY FOR LISA to get the time off at work. Five years and she'd banked all her holidays, working more or less straight through with the odd long weekend here and there. There had been lots of talk of trips abroad with boyfriends, but for various reasons, mostly breakups, they had all fallen through.

We made plans for her to come over for a goodbye dinner the weekend before she was due to leave, but I came home from the market to a message saying she'd already left.

It was a cut-rate, last-minute deal, Sis, she said, in the affable drawl she reserved for my answering machine. My travel agent called and said to go for it. Even with the cancellation fee on the other flight I still saved a ton.

She was flying to London, the starting point for a trip she refused to pin down with places or dates.

That's just fine, I said aloud, emptying the contents of the grocery bags onto the kitchen counter. A solitary green pepper rolled out of reach and dropped to the floor with a hollow thump.

→

IN THE LAST STAGE OF MY FATHER'S ILLNESS, when he knew he was dying, he stopped working.

Taking the oxygen mask from his mouth, he said, I know it's going to be a pain in the neck for you to have to sell off what's left in the store, but I'd rather not be the one to do it.

He was a practical man, but romantic and imaginative enough for the grimness of that final task to get to him. I had offered to take care of it when I'd reaffirmed that I didn't want to carry on the business. He already knew of my disinclination for the trade, so he'd only nodded.

Get your sister to help you, he said. Sell everything to my old favourites.

Dad's old favourites were his regulars, the customers he'd cultivated in his more than forty years in the trade. Mostly older men like himself, though there were a few notable ladies. I came upon his correspondence with the old favourites by chance. It was filed by customer in the tall, dark-green cabinet that occupied the back corner of his office, itself squared away in the store's back quarter. Although some files were comprised only of business transactions, many others contained postcards, Christmas cards, letters of some length exchanged back and forth.

I was impressed by my father's ability to keep up so many prolonged relationships, when I had so far not managed to sustain one. It seemed to me to be the main difference between him and us. His great virtue was constancy, even to our dead mother, who we could barely remember but who he conjured for us as a great woman, a humanist of deep kindness, wit, and beauty.

She was like Grace Kelly, that woman, he said. An air of beauty to everything she did and said. You could hardly believe she was real. Or that she fell for me.

They had met in New York, when he was there for a stamp convention. The fact that she was an American had always made our mother seem bold and exotic to us.

But that was what she was like, he said, no end of surprises about her. She loved boxing, for one thing, that's why you're named Georgie, after George Foreman. She saw him win his first pro fight in New York in a three-round knockout. Hoped you'd turn out a scrapper.

There's still time, I said.

THE POSTCARDS STARTED COMING about a week and a half after she left. Lisa liked to make fun of me for my indefinite delay in joining the electronic age, but I knew she admired it, too. Like many of her co-workers at the centre, she entertained back-to-the-land fantasies of a simpler time: organic farming, goats rambling at whim through long grasses. My internet silence used to strike her as Step One in a healthy disengagement process with modernity, but in one of our last conversations she tried to talk me into email for at least the duration of her trip.

That still wouldn't change the fact that I don't have a computer, I told her. I don't want to get into all that.

The truth was that email made me nervous. There was an expectation of rapidity, the short turnover time between responses, that I wasn't sure I could live up to.

It'll have to be postcards then, she said. You know long letters are pretty much beyond me.

THE FIRST WAS FROM CHARTRES—its famous rose window. *Dear Georgie*, it read. *Every church I see makes me think of you. For the windows alone you should make this trip.* I stuck it to the fridge with a magnet, picture side out.

There were more, from all over Western Europe. She still revealed nothing of her itinerary, if she had one, nor was a planned route discernible from the locations of the postcards. She didn't write much about herself or the people I was sure she'd met, only tidbits related to the pictures, or notes on food she'd tasted. *This latte*, she wrote from Naples, *rivals even the ones from Café Olimpico. You would die and go to heaven.* From Bremen, a photo of a statue, four animals stacked vertically, stiff and tall in bronze. *Do you remember this story?* she wrote. *The Town Musicians? One of the less grim Grimms, I think.*

The frequency of the cards trailed off—unsurprisingly, I thought, given the communication's one-sidedness. I remembered our penpal attempts in childhood and how without exception they were ended by our own neglect. It didn't occur to me to worry. Lisa had taken a year off during her degree to backpack around Great Britain, staying here and there with a few of our father's old favourites, and though she was impulsive and forgetful, she was not inexperienced.

The summer wore on. I took on more commissions, worked longer hours on my projects. Some evenings I bought myself Coronas at the depanneur and drank them on my back porch, reading library novels by the light of a desk lamp trailing outside by an extension cord. I found myself a little surprised by how much I relied on Lisa for occasions to get out of the house, for talk.

I ended up calling Marie-Ève, a woman I knew from a yoga class at the Y. Probably sensing about me some air of social tentativeness, she'd given me her number in case I ever wanted to come out dancing. I found myself in the semi-darkness of a club on St. Laurent, a thick-shouldered man in a rugby shirt downing pints and watching from a pointed distance as I gyrated in a circle with the other women.

Marie-Ève and her friends observed him with glee, prodding me forward with barely concealed giggles. I was persuaded to oblige by sheer amusement at the unabashed girlishness of the whole thing, as well by a drunken glimpse of the man's firm rear end.

He clasped me to him when I approached, leaning in to smell my hair.

You seem nice, he said, breathing hard through his

nose. He tugged me just barely out the front door where I raised my face into the cool of the night breeze. He said, you're a good dancer. He smelled not unpleasantly of beer and unisex cologne. Vetiver, maybe, and musk.

Okay, I said. Then, correcting myself, thanks.

Then he leaned farther across me, heaved over at the waist, and vomited just to the side of the door. I ducked away in time and saw beige flecks spatter the red velvet rope.

Look out, he said, coughing. Sorry.

THE NEXT TIME I HEARD FROM LISA was on the fourth of July, during the first heat wave in which the humidex pushed things to plus forty, securing our civic bragging rights for temperature in both directions. I dragged myself down to Canadian Tire to find almost-emptied shelves where the fans had been, a few others like myself, flat-haired and bleary-eyed, grasping at the remnants. It was as though we'd all only recently awakened to a new season well underway, clutching to our chests the first boxes we could find. I was almost up to the cash before I realized I'd grabbed a mock-Victorian beaded lamp, shoved down to the wrong end of the rack by some desperate customer before me.

I returned home empty-handed, sweat smearing the

ink of Lisa's latest card as I took it from the mailbox. I noticed it had an excess of postage, four stamps across the top instead of one or two, as though she were worried about it not making it to its final destination.

I'm in Ypres, notable for being the first place where the Germans used poison mustard gas. Against Canadian soldiers, too. We must have learned that in history class at some point, but I don't exactly remember. It's been a bit of a sad day trip for me.

Are you having a nice summer? It must be much hotter where you are. Make sure to get out for some of that sunny vitamin D. xoxoxo L.

The picture on the reverse was of a long, lit-up building labelled *Cloth Hall at Night*, windows ranging into the distance to a vanishing point.

ON JULY 25ᵀᴴ, IT WAS BIALYSTOK, also overstamped, a staid shot of the railway station. *There was an uprising in this city,* she wrote, *in the Jewish ghetto. And many, many massacres. Another sad place. How to live among such ghosts? Europeans must all be as stoical as you,* G. And on August 12ᵗʰ, one from Zagreb: *I bet you expected me home before this, didn't you? So did I. But I'm still having a great time. Fingers crossed I don't step on a landmine.*

Having already replaced the main dining room window with a large, geometric fleur-de-lys panel of my own design, I began work on a project for the small side window in the bathroom. I'd toyed with designing something for the kitchen windows over the sink but the tiny room was already short on sunlight. I realized that if left to my own devices I would be inclined to a methodical replacement of all the windows in the house, until at length I'd find myself boxed into a world of colour and filtered light, no way of seeing in or out without tempering the gaze through my own patterns. It was not altogether a comforting thought.

For the bathroom, however, I had long been planning something for a small upper panel topping the main window. Three intertwined roses, viewed side-on, stems trailing through a pearly white background. A nod to the heraldic shield of my father's favourite self-declared country, Rose Island. I'd drawn the initial sketch two years earlier at Lisa's. Though we'd left most of my father's collection at the old store, which felt like a safer place with its grill of iron bars on the windows and door, Lisa had brought home the binder he'd taken to show the nurses on his final trip to the hospital.

BEFORE I EVER BECAME INTERESTED in stained glass, when I was miserable and working as a copy editor in a poisonous office, I took a sick day and spent an afternoon at the store with my father, not long before he stopped working. It was quieter than I'd remembered, probably because Lisa wasn't there, and I watched my father as he went about his usual day, writing letters, preparing packages, checking the auction papers for Ontario, Quebec, and New York. I was struck by the utter tranquility of the place.

It's quiet, I said. There had been only two walk-in customers that day.

My father nodded but warned me about working from home. I had been talking of buying a computer, trying to do the copy-editing thing freelance.

Be careful not to be alone too much, he said, moistening the flap on an envelope. Loneliness rolls in like a fog. And he cast a glance over to his Rose Island binder, as though he had begun to think of himself that way, as a republic unto himself, one of his own creation, miles of ocean between him and the mainland.

I hadn't been careful. In fact, I'd only made adjustments to clear my time for working hours, time I spent toiling in the basement, the only area in my tiny rented house suitable for all the equipment. Once I'd made it my habit to refuse all offers for going out in the evening, there was almost nothing to keep me from working uninterrupted, cutting and grinding and soldering until I noticed sleep creeping over me like a heavy blanket, my limbs becoming stiff and slow like those of an old woman.

I WAS IN THE SHOWER WHEN I GOT the first inkling that something might be wrong. Leaning back to rinse the shampoo from my hair, which seemed all at once to have grown past the base of my neck, I wondered how Lisa managed her thick bangs while she was travelling, if she carried tiny scissors and a hand mirror, or if she was growing them out, brushing them to the side or hiding, half-blind, behind a lengthening fringe. I thought, I should ask her to send me a picture. But there was no way to ask, no return address to post a request to, even if she stayed somewhere long enough to receive one. As the water coasted hot down over my shoulders, I had the sudden realization that for two weeks I had checked the mail every day with a certain expectation of hearing from her, but nothing had come. And it was the twelfth of September, a full month since I'd received her last postcard.

I was on the street in ten minutes, hair still wet, walking at a rapid clip toward Park Avenue and an internet gaming place I'd often passed.

For a free email address, I asked the cashier, a rail-thin

guy slumped on a stool, what's best? Hotmail or something? That was what Lisa had.

He shrugged. Whatever. I like Gmail. He pushed my
money back across the counter. You pay after.

Within five minutes, I had signed up and sent Lisa a
message. *Call me collect*, I finished, *please, right away! Or write
back.* I figured a phone must be as easy to find as a public
computer terminal, no matter where she was. As I stood
up to approach the cash, the guy shook his head.

The minimum charge is fifteen minutes. You might as
well get your money's worth. Then, Okay, okay, whatever,
lady, chill, he said, as I slid the coins at him with a slapshot
flick of the wrist.

FOR TWO DAYS I WAITED for a response, moving like a ghost
through my own life, haunting every action with a new
apprehension. I tried to work but had a panic attack by
the grinder; my chest seared and the glass fell from my
hands as I backed, wobbling, down into a chair. I settled
for cleaning house, scrubbing out the fridge and kitchen
cupboards as a kind of penance and plea. As I lay awake
in bed, I thought, a month isn't that long. She's gone three
weeks before without writing. Sometimes these things
taper off. But I thought, no, the email. Why wouldn't she
have answered that? Then I thought, maybe she's gone

somewhere where she can't find a computer. But where would that be now? Surely not anywhere in Europe.

I thought, maybe she's met someone and run off, somewhere far. Remotest Asia. Maybe she's in love. Please.

By Friday morning I was trembling, with a fear for Lisa but also a dread of my own panic, which I sensed as a kind of brute force ready to overwhelm me. It was September 15th. I hadn't heard anything, though I'd haunted the gaming place until the skinny cashier and I were well acquainted. I had not a clue who to call. Lisa's friends I knew by sight, by first name, by any number of anecdotes, but I could not think of a single number or even why I would have occasion to know one. Holly popped to mind, but I had never heard her last name. And then I knew at once who I could call, the man whose name I'd heard so much that his sudden absence through these long months was almost as pointed as my sister's. He was in the phone book.

I dialed his number.

Hello? His voice was fluid, a baritone, softer than I'd expected.

Hi, is this Will?

Lisa? he asked. His voice got ten pegs louder, but I barely registered the volume as I realized he hadn't been in touch with her. There was a frantic note in his tone, a pleading. I wondered if anyone would ever utter my name with the same longing.

Lisa, he repeated, I've been calling and calling.

No, sorry. This is Lisa's sister, Georgia.

Oh, he said. Hello. You sound just like her.

So I've been told, I said. Apparently we also look alike and have the same handwriting. Nervous babble.

Is she okay? he asked. Where is she? She hasn't responded to any of my emails. She's away, isn't she?

Actually, that's why I'm calling. He listened as I explained, and I could hear the heaviness of his breath through the line, could imagine my face moistening with each of his exhalations, tensed to the transparent rigidity of a pane of glass.

Oh no, he said. No. Oh God. There was a long pause. She's missing, he said.

I guess, I said. Yes.

WE MET AT A COFFEE SHOP down the street from my place. I made sure to get there first, as I didn't want to be the one angling around on arrival. I was sipping a lukewarm cup of tea when he walked in and made straight for me, without hesitation. The confidence of a very handsome man.

Hi Georgia, he said. You're the spitting image. He

was tall, dark-haired and obviously fit, notably well-shod in Italian leather loafers. His green eyes zeroed in on me and for a moment I thought he would lean in for an embrace, the European greeting standard even among some Anglophones in Montreal. But I sat back down, pushing the last three postcards across the table toward him.

That's a lot of stamps, he noted.

Yes, I said. What do you think? What should I do? Do I call the police?

Will studied the postmarks, squinting to read the dates.

I think it's the Canadian consulate, actually, he said, in the country we last know her to have been in. Or Foreign Affairs or something. When was she due to come back?

I don't know, I said. She had an open-jaw ticket for London. No fixed plans.

He frowned. That could make things difficult in convincing them she's actually missing, but I'm sure they'll begin an investigation. They can probably trace her passport, see where she made her last border crossing. If necessary, I think we can get the banks to monitor her accounts, her credit cards, let us know where she makes a purchase.

Oh. It all seemed obvious. I could feel my lip tremble

as I let out a breath. Will gave me a faint smile.

Listen, he said, eyes serious. I'm sure it'll be fine. Of course you're frantic. I am, too. But I'll help you get the ball rolling. I'll do everything I can. I've been worried for weeks with no outlet.

Right, I said. Okay. Lisa is just spacing out. She does that sometimes.

Over the next week, Will came over every day at mid-morning, dressed in his work clothes, dark suit and tie. I still had only a vague idea of what he did as having something to do with investment banking. He'd dismissed it as uninteresting, intimating that he was his own boss, free to leave the office as necessary.

He'd shrug out of his jacket in the hall, join me in the kitchen where I'd be sitting at the table, making notes, or still on hold with an embassy or government office.

Where are we at? he'd say, and I'd tell him. I'd called every hostel in Zagreb and hadn't found one where Lisa had registered. Possibly she'd stayed with friends. Foreign Affairs was making inquiries, but didn't have a lot to go on. I couldn't even confirm where she may have been headed after Croatia.

At the end of the week, Will took the notebook from my hands and paged through it, face grim. I'm getting about ready, he said, if you don't mind, to begin throwing money at this.

WILL TOOK OVER with a charged efficiency.

I don't want you to feel weird, he said. Trust me that Lisa is a firm believer in letting people pay for what they can afford, and I can afford this.

He hired private detectives and paid a web developer to mount a site that would log all tips and comments. He also cross-posted a public appeal on dozens of blogs and back-packer message boards, screening all responses and emails for useful information.

I continued to spend the days making calls and filing reports with police departments across Europe. In the evenings, I headed into the basement and let myself go in a flurry of work, which I found was the only kind of absorption that could stave off grief. I had the thought that with enough money I could fly to Europe and look for her myself, turning over rocks, shouting her name in the streets.

Every day at four he called to check in. He called it our summit meeting. I reflected, in spite of myself, that Will seemed almost compulsively reliable, not at all as Lisa had described. He went at the search with a ferocity I couldn't quite understand, which rattled my faith in the depth of my own feelings for Lisa, for he had an unwavering belief that she was alive. I tried to share in his certainty, but couldn't, at least not with any consistency.

Listen, if she were dead you would know, he said. I could hear the clicks and whirring of office machines in the background, laser printers spitting out pages.

I was not as convinced of the sanctity of our connection, recalling a time I'd fallen off my bike at the park and knocked myself unconscious. I woke up in the dark to my father leaning over me, nervous and relieved. Lisa had returned home oblivious, assuming I'd headed home on my own, and between them it had taken an hour to notice I was missing.

All I said to Will was, I think all that stuff is a bunch of bull. How could I possibly know?

SOMEWHERE IN ALL THIS was when the comics went missing, when Daniel came over to take the report and I collapsed into tears. The way it broke me down made me realize I needed to do more, even if everything was already being done. It occurred to me to mail the posters Will had had printed to my father's old favourites. Though not all of them were in the general vicinity of where we supposed Lisa to be, the truth was that she could be anywhere. It was the closest thing I had to a global network.

The shop was dustier than I'd expected. There was another letter in the mail from the neighbourhood improvement group, urging us to consider leasing the property to a new owner with a viable business plan. It was something to think about; the place was rapidly becoming an eyesore. All that Lisa and I had done in the past five years was maintain an uninterrupted policy of denial and neglect.

I slid open the top drawer of the ancient filing cabinet where my father had kept the typed master list of customers. With his instinct for the endurance of physical objects, he'd oiled the drawers so they slid like a dream. The folder had a thin stack of lists right at the front, dating back to five years before my father closed up shop. Since he had no computer, my father kept scrupulous paper records.

The most recent list was missing, though, and I wondered whether it had been misplaced during the final online auction when Lisa had disposed of most of the remaining contents of the store. She had borrowed it so she could advertise and urge the old favourites to get online for bidding. They'd done it, too, cleaned out the inventory and left us with an above-market-value return, a sum we'd more or less ignored as we had ignored the store, Dad's personal collection, and, to a certain degree, I supposed, our total aloneness in the world.

Settling for the second-most recent list, which was six years old, I sat at my father's work table and began addressing envelopes, tracing the pen across the manila with a feeling finally approaching optimism. My cell phone rang. It was Will.

There's some news, he said. We can narrow the search. Lisa definitely went to England.

THE NEWS ABOUT THE DOVER STAMP on Lisa's passport was encouraging for a time, but it didn't take long to realize that there had been no news of her for over two months since the border crossing. She had entered the United Kingdom on August 5, even before I'd received her last postcard.

Daniel, who had begun coming round every fourth or fifth night with offerings of beer and pastries, thought the news was encouraging.

The British police are supposed to be amazing, aren't they? he said. And now at least we know she went missing in a place where the people speak English.

We don't know anything, I said, louder than I'd meant to, and Daniel was quiet.

All through this time Daniel kept a careful distance,

always sitting in the far chair and leaving me the couch, or, if we were outside, giving me the lawn chair while he leaned up against the porch rail. Daniel was willing to discuss Lisa, but he began to gauge my moods and sometimes offer up little kernels of distraction, police anecdotes or stories about growing up on a farm in Saskatchewan with four brothers. I had an idea he was moved by my situation, his Good Samaritanness so well engrained that he couldn't find a way to stop himself from coming over. I felt as though he treated me with the kind consideration due an invalid aunt, or perhaps a sister.

One evening, after hopping up unasked to fetch me a glass of water then returning to his chair on the opposite side of the room, he was startled when I snapped at him.

What are even you doing here? I asked.

THE NEXT AFTERNOON WHEN WILL called for our summit meeting, I invited him over for dinner.

It's the least I can do, I said. Please.

He showed up early, as I was making the salad, with two bottles of wine, one white and one red.

I didn't know what you liked, he said. He ran his fingers through his dark hair, as though still undecided.

You do too much, I said, scolding. That's what this is all about.

Will shook his head. Nothing is too much for Lisa, he said. I was forced to agree.

He sat at the tiny kitchen table as I prepared the food, after I'd turned down his offer to help. Mixing the dressing, I looked over and admired how he'd managed to curl his large frame into the low chair, his long legs stretched out to the side and his forearm resting along the table's edge, fingers curled on the stem of his glass.

So what went wrong with you and Lisa? I asked as I put the pasta on to boil.

He looked pained but not offended.

The fact is that I'm a very private person, he said. Always have been. It isn't easy for the women I date, but there's not much I can do.

I see, I said. I pulled out a chair and sat down.

I'm jealous of my time, too, he said. I like to work. I take pleasure in it. He nodded toward my fleur-de-lys window. I'm sure you know what I mean, being an artist. It's hard. It feels selfish. But I'm not sure what the alternative is, if you have things you need to accomplish.

I nodded. I said, I love the feeling of an afternoon stretching out in front of me, with nothing to do except work on something for as long as it takes. Letting the day run on into the night.

Absorption, he said. Exactly.

Will pushed his glass ahead, leaning forward to cross his arms on the table. I wish we could have left things on better terms, Lisa and I, he said. That we could have found a way to make it work. But she came to a decision, and there wasn't anything I could do about that. I stopped making promises I couldn't keep a long time ago.

He looked rueful. I had never heard him say so much at once, least of all about himself.

Well, Lisa's not one to hold a grudge, I told him. Or even remember a grudge. She's a bit scatterbrained like that. Tears began to glaze my eyes then and I stood up, turning to stir the pasta. Conjuring Lisa to him almost felt like nostalgia, or giving up.

Are you okay? he asked. He half-rose from his seat.

I swiped at my face with my shirt sleeve. I thought I was all cried out, I said, and Will took a step toward me.

It seemed to me at that moment that if I had let him, he would have held me. But I turned back again to stir the pasta, even though by then it would have boiled itself just fine on its own.

Will invited me over for dinner two days later.

It's my turn, he said. I'd like to cook for you.

I showed up late, in a black dress and with a rapid pulse I told myself was from hurrying to catch the bus.

He uncorked a bottle of white wine and poured me a glass, then filled one for himself. I looked around his open-concept kitchen, at the stainless steel appliances and dark wood cabinets that Lisa must have admired as well. It might have seemed to her that, unlike her other lovers, Will would not need to take anything from her. Then again, that kind of material appraisal seemed never to enter her mind.

Do you like it? asked Will. He was watching me.

Oh, definitely. Of course. It's beautiful. I took another look, casting my gaze farther, over the breakfast island to the living room beyond with its leather couches, gas fireplace, and checkerboard rug. There was a glassed-in bookcase, too, full of trade paperbacks, rows and rows of novels and even a few slim volumes that looked like poetry. In the corner, by a carved teak magazine rack, was the missing milk crate full of Archie comics. I looked back at Will.

What are you doing with that? I asked. My voice came out sharp. Will blinked and put down his wine glass.

With what? Oh, that. He looked over at the crate. Right. Yeah, sorry.

What are you doing with that? I repeated.

I just borrowed it a while ago to look for clues. I remembered you telling me it was Lisa's.

You just came over and took it? What the hell?

He gave me a funny, even look. I just borrowed it, Georgia. I knocked, popped my head in. You were downstairs, I guess. There was some equipment going. I didn't want to scare you by interrupting. I figured I'd call and tell you about it later.

Well, you fucking didn't tell me, I said. I thought somebody stole it. I called the fucking police, you asshole.

I'm sorry, he said, approaching. You never told me. He put his hands on my shoulders, bending his knees slightly to lock eyes. I am so, so sorry. I had no idea it had been missed. I completely forgot I'd walked off with it without asking. Please believe me, Georgia, I would never intentionally cause you pain.

His hands cupped my cheeks, tilting my face up toward him. With his right hand, he stroked my hair. For a moment, I leaned into the touch, my mouth slackening, my eyes closing before going wide and yielding with what might have looked like gratitude, for Will was gazing back at me with a kind of benevolence.

Is this okay? he asked.

What are you doing? I said, jerking my head upright,

still in his hands.

His voice was soft. I think we both deserve a little comfort, after everything we've been through. Don't you?

I stepped back. Stop it, I said.

He looked at me. Okay. But I'm not sure what you think is wrong about this.

Then you're not being honest.

We stared at each other.

I want to show you something, he said at length, crooking an eyebrow. I nodded and followed him to his office, to a black wooden desk, empty except for a sleek laptop he booted up.

The last email I got from Lisa, he said.

Will, I don't know how you guessed, but yes, I'm pregnant. What's more, I'm never giving up this baby.

You see, he said, I think she's hiding from me.

He was looking at me again, with an appraising eye. So you didn't know, he said.

No, I said. And again, after a pause: no.

I'm sorry I didn't tell you, he said. But this is why I'm sure she's alive. She sent this the day you said she left. I wanted to tell you, but—well, I guess I didn't want you to blame me. As he stood, he squeezed the back of the desk chair, his broad shoulders straining forward toward the computer screen, his chin lifting. And I don't even know how Lisa got the idea I would want her to get rid of the baby. I would have supported her totally. I knew she would never have an abortion. I knew that before we even got together. It was a conversation we had.

That's true, I said. She wouldn't.

I guess she thought, maybe because of, well, the circumstances of our relationship, that I would be upset that she was pregnant.

You mean because of Holly? I asked, watching his face.

Yes. He sighed. So you do blame me. But I'm not ashamed. I was honest with them. It's a perfectly legitimate way to be in the world.

That may be, I said. But I've got to go.

I FOUND THE THIEF, I said, when he picked up.

Hey, said Daniel. I'm glad you called. Was it a kid?

Nope. My sister's ex-boyfriend.

Huh. I guess they always tell you to check out the ex-boyfriends first.

It was a misunderstanding.

I see. Well, I'm glad it's been sorted out. I'll call off my surveillance of the boys next door.

Please do.

—

I ALLOWED MYSELF A SMALL BUBBLE of hope based on Will's revelation and began drafting a notice to run in the international papers. The only thing that had changed, it seemed to me, was that Lisa's tragedy had been superficially compounded. She had become a missing pregnant woman instead of only a missing woman, though I could not feel any additional hope or despair for an unborn child. But if Lisa was really just afraid of being pressured into an abortion, if she was really only in hiding, there was no reason not to come home. *Dear Lisa,* I wrote, *He doesn't want you to get rid of it.* It sounded blunt, but I didn't know how else to put it. *We both miss you.* Then, thinking that sounded too chummy, I changed it to *Everyone misses you. Come back.*

It seemed an age since she had left. It had been spring when she'd flown to London, and now it was fall, the rain heavy and continual. When I took the shortcut through the park, the ground oozed beneath my feet like a soaked sponge, running out into new gluts and streams. I counted on my fingers and discovered that if Lisa had been pregnant when she left, she'd already be big, obvious. I could not think how she could be concealing herself. It seemed like too much of a miracle to suppose that she was not only alive, but also realizing her dream of becoming a mother. England was not that big a place.

I felt, too, as though my raggedness was becoming apparent. I slept in my clothes, lived on takeout and granola bars. When I walked my lamps over to the boutiques that sold them, the shop owners handed over cheques without raising their eyes, never introducing me as the artist, as they sometimes used to if a customer was eyeing a lamp while I was there.

It was the mornings, with their stark and glaring newness, when I despaired of Lisa. At night I could more easily believe that she had spirited herself away by choice. It wasn't that I thought of myself as someone who would be difficult to leave. If anything, the opposite.

LISA AND I USED TO MAKE A HABIT of going for long walks on the weekend, beginning at my place and spinning south, through back alleys and main drags, turning left and right by caprice, our only destination an acceptable version of somewhere else. This brought us by turns to the Plateau, to Old Montreal with its cobblestones and loud American accents, or to Westmount with its unfathomable lives. Sitting down for a rest on a park bench was a mutual acknowledgement that we'd arrived and would soon turn back, usually to another two- or three-hour walk, accounting for window shopping and wrong turns. Invariably, once we'd sat but never earlier, I'd be hit by exhaustion, notice the pain in my calves or a fresh blister, and I'd delay our return, point out a nearby restaurant where we could stop for a snack or coffee, or suggest the bus.

Lisa's disappearance reminded me of this lull at the midpoint of our walks, the feeling it brought about as I took stock of how far we'd ventured and what was yet to come. At these times, she was still buoyant, and I flailed with dismay. The reprieve, the suspension of self-awareness she cast over me in the movement to and fro, was unique to my walks with her, even when we fell into silence together. I knew that wherever Lisa was, whether lost or hidden or dead, she carried her oblivion with her, the forgetfulness that permitted joy and easy action, that shielded her from pain—her own and that of other people. And that without her, her absence would be hard to survive.

DANIEL CALLED ON A SATURDAY NIGHT and suggested we go out.

Out where? I asked, surprised. Though I'd called to tell him about the comic collection, I hadn't seen him in two weeks, since the day we'd found out about Lisa's passport.

You know, out. For drinks. Out on the town.

At the bar, Daniel was relaxed and attentive, going

through beers quickly. It was crowded, so we sat close to each other, at stools along the bar. At points I noticed his knee edging closer as he spoke, his arm nudging mine for emphasis, and I was feeling better than I had in ages, or at least drunker, when I excused myself to use the toilet.

On the way to the bathroom, I almost tripped over a woman sitting on the floor with her legs stuck out, back planted against a pillar. Looking down, I saw that it was Holly, hair dampened flat to her skull, forehead glistening. Her eyes were half-closed, eyelids shimmering gold and dusty rose.

Holly, I said, bending to her.

Lisa, she said, grabbing my arm. Then, searching my eyes, oh. No. Um.

It's Georgia, I said.

Hi, how are you? She struggled to her feet, good manners superseding what appeared to be a drunken crisis. She rocked a little on the kitten heels of her pointed black shoes, finding her balance. Have you heard from Lisa lately? she asked. She smoothed some strands of hair back out of her face then wiped her palms on the thighs of her dark cigarette pants. When is she getting back?

Hearing this, my throat tightened.

Not sure, I said. How have you been?

Holly let out an exaggerated sigh, hugging her bare arms. She had an air of amused resignation. Oh, who knows? she said. Then added, every time I see you I'm a mess. You must think I'm nuts.

You seemed fine when I saw you before.

She shook her head. I met you the day I went to the clinic, she said. Met you and rushed off. Before Lisa went away. She lowered her voice, adopting the air of conspiratorial revelation peculiar to intoxication. It was the day I had my abortion. I was a wreck.

Oh, I said. Oh, geez.

Yeah, she nodded. Anyway, I'm sorry we didn't get to talk more that day.

She smiled at me, looking grateful, and squeezed my upper arm. Her head dropped back to rest against the pillar, eyes focusing on the ceiling where the lights for the dance floor rotated, flashing in bursts of colour.

Will, she said. Will is a maniac. Did Lisa ever tell you?

Will, I said. Really.

A total fiend. I mean, he's a fucking psycho. He's married, for one thing. That's something he keeps under wraps. And when he found out I was pregnant, he tried to buy me off. Offered me like a hundred thousand dollars to have the baby and then hand it over. Pretend I never existed.

I stared. You're kidding. Holly looked up at me and kept her head going in a vigorous nod, even as she rooted with both hands in the gold quilted purse slung over one shoulder. She took out a tube of lip gloss and began applying it with her ring finger.

Yeah, no, I'm serious. I only told him because I figured he ought to help pay for the abortion. Holly pressed her lips together, tracing with the edge of her finger around her bottom lip. She tilted her head closer. And you know, it got me thinking maybe he tampered with my birth control, because honestly what are the chances? They say it's less than one percent. So fucking twisted. And his wife. He said her infertility was causing tensions so she took a job in New York. She's a family lawyer, apparently. Who could make an adoption go through like *that*. She snapped her fingers. I blinked.

I don't know what to say, I said. That's crazy. I can't believe it.

I know, eh? I was telling Lisa all this the day we saw you, she said. I felt like she ought to know.

Yeah, I said. Wow.

It was raining again as we left the club. Daniel tried to follow me to my door with an umbrella.

Rain check on that nightcap? I asked. He nodded.

But you look spooked, he said.

It's fine, I said. I'll tell you later.

I SAT AT THE KITCHEN TABLE with Lisa's last postcard, thinking about Holly and everything she had said, about the jolt of finding someone who still believed Lisa to be on her way home, and the odd comfort of yet another person who could confuse us by sight. It was strange to have a sister so much like myself. Glancing at the postcard, it was easy to imagine it was something I had written myself and forgotten. It was like coming upon an old grocery list scribbled somewhere, for a recipe impossible to recall. It was the same thing growing up in the same house as her, always the eerie doubling without mirrors, though at times it offered a handy insight into what I might look like from otherwise inaccessible angles.

It was a principle I had taken too far. Based on Lisa's experiments, I'd passed over all kinds of possibilities: perms, blue eyeliner, gaucho pants. Once I'd seen what something might be like on me, it didn't seem worth trying. Blonde highlights. Gymnastics. Certain kinds of friends. Certain kinds of men.

Thinking of Will, then, of the unexpected broadness of his chest, the way his hands and jaw had a hard look of readiness about them in spite of his soft eyes and mouth, the seeming gentility of his manners. Holly's strange accusations. When I forced these thoughts out, I let my eyes refocus on the postcard and on Lisa's handwriting, so much like my own, the swirls of rounded letters in a thick, black ink. And then I saw it.

It was the farthest left of the stamps, completely redundant postage-wise, untouched by the postmark. I couldn't believe I'd missed it, accustomed as I was to scanning stamps, to taking them in at a glance. I had to suppose I'd been too eager to read what she had to say, before sticking it to the fridge so that the photo of the cathedral showed. I hurried to the fridge and retrieved the previous two postcards, laying them out chronologically across the table.

Three postcards and three of the Rose Island stamps, one from each series, each tagged on to the end of a row of excessive postage, the extra stamps meant perhaps not only to spare the collectibles from the postmark, but also to draw attention away from their very strangeness. Clues in plain sight. The place names, too, seemed to indicate something once I started looking at them: Ypres, Bialystok, Zagreb. A gravity weighted toward the end of the alphabet, toward some kind of finish.

WILL MADE ARRANGEMENTS for us to meet at the coffee shop, astutely aware of the need for neutral ground. There had been a restraint between us since I found him with the comics, but this time it was all I could do to hide my new unease as I conducted a covert moral appraisal, judging every change in intonation, watching his face for some kind of canniness or sly look.

Between us, we took stock again of our findings, all the leads we'd followed and ruled out. No bank activity, no email activity. The last place Lisa had logged in was Zagreb, where she'd sent some chatty and uninformative notes to a few friends. No trace of her, according to any of her known acquaintances, since I'd received the last postcard. No trace found anywhere by Will's detectives or the authorities. There had been lots of tips posted on the website, but none that had panned out. She had been missing for eighty-two days.

She made a large withdrawal before she left, I said, looking at the copied bank statement.

True. Will's head tilted to the side in a minute shift from assessment to dismissal. But not so large that she wouldn't have already run through it.

Lisa's thrifty, though, I said. She hates banks and banking fees. Will shrugged, and I remembered that he might be a banker, of some variety.

On the bright side, he said, looking dispassionate, his eye twitching a little as he rubbed it, none of her belongings have turned up, her passport, nothing. So no signs of foul play.

I nodded. The mixture of gratitude and revulsion that I felt for him, the lust and reproach, had paralyzed me with doubt. Like an ailing climber midway to the summit, laid low by the altitude, I was caught between hope and a physical instinct. But there was no way to confirm his motivations, to discover if he would be helping me, helping Lisa, if he had nothing at stake. I felt that if I could just know this one thing, then everything else, the baseness of his love life, his scruples, whether morally advanced or merely selfish, would become only details, the scaffolding and not the foundation upon which to assess his character. But, like always, I could see no way in, no reliable way to bridge the gulf between person and person with absolute transparency.

Well, that's it for now, then, he said. We'll just keep plugging away.

I watched him as he left, shirt stretched grey and smooth across his back, the dipping V of its western stitching like a child's drawing of a bird in flight. His long legs moved with rapid purpose to carry him away.

THE MESSAGE OF THE STAMPS was not altogether clear. The stages of the Republic of Rose Island, as I could recall them, were its creation, its occupation by the Italian authorities and the exile of its inhabitants, and its eventual demolition by the Italian army. By all accounts, if you looked out across the water from Rimini, you would no longer see any trace of the brief, invented country or even of its ruined concrete supports.

Lisa had mailed them in order. The Ypres card bore the first stamp, with its aerial view of Italy, a dot just off the northeast coast of the country marking Rose Island's location in the Adriatic Sea, a superimposed sketch of Rosa's covered platform in the corner. The second stamp in the series, affixed to the back of Bialystok's train station, was the same, only marked with a black-inked rubber stamp, a box with text inside translating to *Italian Military Occupation*. The last, from Zagreb, was a picture of an explosion: the structure surrounded by a cloud of smoke, a yellow fireball in the centre of the image blasting apart the platform and its nine pillars embedded in the sea. Issued by Giorgio Rosa as a last, defiant tribute to his project.

I refused at once to interpret the explosion as a symbol for any kind of self-destruction. If Lisa became suicidal, it would be an event. Someone would spot her, clinging to a bridge rail, or there would be a note, a letter with woes so freely confessed that it would lighten her own heart, staving off the act. Lisa could only have sent herself away, into exile, and since Lisa did things thoroughly, she had confided in no one, with only these tiny, secret hints, themselves like a rehearsal of disappearance, to say goodbye.

I RAN IT ALL BY DANIEL, who had taken to holding my hand, his shirt sleeves rolled up on his days off, the yellow hair on his forearms long and straight like the hair of a terrier. He had the earthy skepticism of his farming family, what he called his built-in bullshit detector, but also a frank anticipation, an inborn way of looking forward in hope that I attributed to a reliance on natural rhythms and harvests. He called my rural stereotyping a cute affectation, and usually played along, mulling the problems I put to him with his supposedly uncorrupted instincts.

I can't fathom it one way or the other, he said, meaning the stamps and whether Lisa's disappearance might be intentional. I could tell he didn't want to get my hopes up.

On the subject of Will, he was less puzzled. He said, there's no law that a fine face is a fine heart. Except in my case, of course.

I didn't remember telling Daniel that Will was good-looking, though I must have, and he must have filed that fact away as being one of utmost relevance, as, in fact, it was.

Mostly, I said, letting myself register the consolation of Daniel's touch, his presence beside me, I'm not sure what to do next. If I believe Lisa doesn't want to be found, is it my duty to stop looking? Or as her only family am I bound to an unending search?

I wondered if I sounded whiny. I was concerned by Daniel's ability to listen and remember; what evidence of my character would he take away from this?

I could sell the store, I said, or rent it out. Go look for her myself.

Would you have more luck than professional detectives? asked Daniel. I shrugged.

You could run the store, he said. Reopen it under a new name and sell your own stuff there.

What does that have to do with anything? I asked. Daniel's face was a mixture of care and cautious encouragement. It was bewildering how at every turn he was ready, prepared to accept my wild gamut of emotions.

If you're going to wait for her to come home, he said, it'll be better if you have something to do.

—

TWO WEEKS LATER AND I WAS STILL WAITING, hoping for something to break, some news. I spent the mornings carrying out tasks related to the search, afternoons at my father's store, going through the items that remained. I came home in darkness to head down into my workshop.

She's alive, Will told my answering machine one evening. She's alive, and I've left you the proof.

In my mailbox I found a postcard, addressed to Will, with a photo of a sandy beach, a Jamaican stamp and postmark. In familiar swirling, black-inked cursive, it read, *Will, I lost the baby. I figured you deserve to know this. I'm okay, I've made friends and they're taking care of me. I feel like a bit of an ass for the way I left everything, but you know I freak out sometimes. Tell Georgia I love her even though I'm sure she knows. Peace. Lisa.*

I guess she just didn't want to be found, said Will. His voice on the message crackled with irritation, clipped and harsh. And I have to say I'm not entirely convinced you didn't know that. Although I'd prefer to believe you didn't let me spend a fortune trying to seek her out just for your own amusement.

I read the card over, rubbing my thumb over my handiwork, the first sentence meant to discourage, the last ones expressing what I wished rather than believed to be true. I'd mailed it in an envelope to an old favourite in Kingston, requesting that she post it to Will from her hometown.

That's it, then, I said aloud.

IN STAMP COLLECTING, WHAT TURN OUT to be most valuable are the mistakes. I remembered our father schooling me in some famous examples: the Inverted Jenny, with the biplane printed upside-down on early U.S. stamps; or, more recently, the Canadian Christmas issues with the dieresis misplaced on *Noël*, thirty million recalled but the ones that escaped fetching huge sums at auction. It occurred to me that if Lisa came back I would tell her about this backward principle of values. I'd tell her, and I'd remind myself at the same time.

The baby, if there was one, I would only hold, marvelling at how Lisa had made something out of nothing.

BY CHRISTMAS, WILL HAD JOINED HIS WIFE in New York, at least according to Holly, who I ran into again and who admitted to occasional strolls past his old apartment. By that time the advertisement had been running for two months, since the point when I could almost be sure he had pulled his detectives off the case.

I have been running it for a year in every paper in

Britain, no matter how small, and in other places, too, anywhere an old favourite might have taken her under a wing for my father's sake. *Dear Betty,* it begins, *Don't worry about Archie. He's out of the picture and he's left Riverdale.*

In time, it might be safe to speak plainly. But since she chose to hide, to vanish into cipher, I am only hoping that I can prove my mettle, my willingness to play along. To opt for hope, and, like her, to disappear into my own life, instead of only into myself.

When Lisa comes home, Daniel and I will get married. And if we are called upon to talk about how we met, to tell the story, Lisa will be there to hear it—to nod her head in approbation, or to quibble, or simply to interject.

The White Dress

OUR HOUSE WAS ALWAYS COLD. Linnie liked to leave the window open. She thought the night air would make us healthier, our lungs bigger, our skins thicker. It was like what Garek said the Spartans did with their babies, bathing them in wine instead of water to make them tougher, to root out the weak ones. Or like Mrs. Gavranovic from up the street always said, that what doesn't kill you will only make you stronger. But I was worried the night air would come in and freeze my bones and find me lacking and I would never get warm again. That Linnie and Garek would decide they didn't want me after all, and they'd leave me out on a mountain to die alone, like the weak Spartan babies. Exposed. I was terrified of being exposed.

But I only felt this fear at night, when the hot-water bottle tucked between my sheets had lost its heat and the tip of my nose was cold and I couldn't get it warm again. One of my favourite things to tell Linnie was that she should knit me a nosewarmer, which I pictured as being shaped like a miniature toque or a nightcap just about the size of my baby finger and with its own little pompom on the end.

Linnie was always saying she was going to learn how to knit, just like she was going to learn how to make jam and pickles. Garek said she was trying to cultivate country traditions, even though we lived in the city. She bought preserves and quilts and rag rugs at craft shows and country fairs. I didn't know why we needed to make our own pickles, because it was just as easy to buy them, but I was starting to learn that people placed more value on things they made themselves, which is why being adopted wasn't as good as being somebody's own child. Sometimes I would picture Linnie buying me at the fair, picking out the white bundle on the table beside rows of gleaming jewel-toned jellies. A grey-haired lady wrapping me up in newspaper next to the Mason jars.

The hot-water bottle itself was one point on which Linnie didn't get her way. Linnie wanted to bake bricks in the oven and then wrap them in towels, because that's what they used to do in the olden days, but Garek told her not to be ridiculous, that the whole point of progress was not to have to fill your daughter's bed with hot rocks. So instead I got the pink rubber bottle, wrapped up in a yellow gingham dishcloth that was thick enough to keep me from burning my toes when it first went in but thin enough to let the heat through. The trick was managing to fall asleep right away, your feet pressed up on either side of the bottle while it was still warm. Sometimes I could do it, but more often I laid awake for what seemed to be a long time, thinking.

The night I first saw the book was a cold night too, especially for July. I remember lying in bed afterward, shivering beneath the crow's-foot quilt, making the black and orange triangles quiver. I turned over and pulled my knees to my chest under the thin cotton of my yellow nightgown. I had started looking at words, and *nightgown* was a funny one. When I thought of gowns, I pictured flowing dresses with frills and bows and yards of glossy silk. But a nightgown, my nightgown at least, was just the opposite, straight and plain with two white buttons at the top. In a way it made sense to me, when I thought about the difference between night and day and the gap between who people seemed to be and who they really were in their secret selves when no one else was around.

I felt like a different girl in the solitude of my bed from the one I was when I played outside in the yard in the daytime. As the night air blew about my face, I watched the glow from passing cars beam travelling patches of light across my bed and the shadowed ceiling, and I thought more about my mother and about the book.

I had seen her writing in it before bed. Garek was away up north on business, doing work for the Department of Indian Affairs. He was helping bring education to poor Indian children who lived in the forest and didn't know how to read. I'd offered to send my extra copy of *Alice in Wonderland* and, with some reluctance, my blue pup tent, but he said it was his job to get the children out of the bush and into nice warm schools where they wouldn't need my little tent. But he'd kissed me on the forehead then and said I was a princess for offering.

Linnie and I had dinner alone that night, and she sent me to bed early. I woke up and heard two cats fighting outside on the street below my window. All the wailing and hissing sounded like the cries of babies being attacked by snakes, and I ran into the master bedroom, wearing my quilt like a cloak. Linnie was sitting up in bed, writing in a book with a green pen. When she saw me, she closed the book up with her pen inside it and placed it into the drawer of her bedside table. She spoke to me only after she had done this.

"Hello, Shay darling," she said, and she held out her arm and pulled back the bedspread next to her. So I crawled in and told her about the sounds I'd heard, and she told me it was probably only Mrs. Gavranovic's old tomcat showing the new tabby on the street who was boss.

I allowed myself to be comforted, wriggling my cold feet toward the warmth of Linnie's legs. But I wasn't thinking so much about the cats now as about the book. I closed my eyes and sighed. I had never seen Linnie writing before, nothing beyond grocery lists or pages of sample letters with which I practiced my printing. But just as I was beginning to drift into sleep, Linnie touched my shoulder and told me to go back to bed. Even though Garek was away, she thought it was important for me to sleep in my own room. So I went. The Spartans also raised their children to never fear the darkness, and maybe that was Linnie's way of thinking, too.

So I was considering the book as I lay on my side in my bed, palm tucked beneath my ear against the pillow. I wondered if it would be possible to sneak into my parents' bedroom without waking them up. It was a bold idea, a nighttime idea. The kind of idea that made me wonder if children really could be returned after all, like a rotten tomato or a spoiled jar of jam. One time my mother took an apron back to the fair where she'd bought it, its seams collapsing from a loose thread, the apron reduced to squares of flowered cotton before she'd even got it home.

IN THE MORNING, I THOUGHT OF THE BOOK right away. The sunlight was pouring through the window, picking out the spots on the bedspread where the unknown quilter had used golden thread to outline the patches of black cotton.

What had struck me was Linnie's manner when I'd surprised her in her writing. The care she had taken to put the book away, her focus on it instead of me, even as I slid with all speed across the floor toward her. And the rapid movement of her wrist as she pulled open the drawer, the speed with which she stowed the book inside. It pointed to concealment, if not to guilt.

I thought of the summer before, when Mim, the girl down the street, found me singing Christmas carols to myself in the back yard. I'd been trying to memorize the extra verses to "We Three Kings of Orient Are," the ones that never got sung in church but that I'd found in an old hymn book that used to belong to Linnie's mother, Mrs. Almead. I loved the verse about myrrh, and

I was trying to do justice to its creepiness by singing it as gloomily as possible. In my deepest voice I was droning, "Sealed in the stone-cold tomb!" when I heard Mim behind me saying hello. I dropped the book and turned and sat on it, telling Mim that I hadn't been singing or doing anything at all, really. Part of me knew Mim would think it was weird to sing Christmas carols in July, but more than that, I didn't want to share the myrrh verse with her. Now I knew that whatever Linnie had in that book was as special to her as the myrrh verse was to me.

Linnie's secrecy had given her a whole new dimension for me. I had a basic idea of Linnie based on the fact of my adoption and the simple, fairy-tale way it had been described to me. Before I was adopted, Linnie and Garek, but Linnie especially, were very sad because they weren't able to have any children. I liked to think of her like this, going to the park or the store and seeing other parents with their little children and filled with a sad, desperate wish. I liked to think about it because of its happy ending, because of the way my own existence became the salvation of Linnie's happiness. I got her to tell me the story so many times that she finally refused to ever tell it to me again.

"You're insatiable," she said, turning away from me and back to the tomatoes she was transplanting into the garden. There was a row of little green pots lined up between us, one of them already empty and overturned, its fragile former tenant tucked snugly into the dark earth. The sky overhead was cloudy that day, as Linnie said it ought to be for transplanting tomatoes, but I could not stop myself from looking up to check on it every few minutes, just in case I needed to call a stop to the whole operation.

AFTER LUNCH, I WAITED UNTIL LINNIE was on the telephone, pressing the cream-coloured receiver against her ear and tracing light circles over her forehead. Her voice was hushed in the way it always was during her daily call to Mrs. Almead, whom I had only met once because she lived far away in a place called the prairies. Linnie said her mother didn't like talking on the phone, which is why she never put me on to speak to her. But I wondered why, if Mrs. Almead didn't like talking on the phone, she made Linnie call her every day, and why Linnie always looked as though she were having one of her headaches during their conversations. I kept out of the way during these calls, for Linnie would wave me away with a frown if I didn't.

I slipped upstairs into my parents' bedroom and went to Linnie's bedside table. I tugged on the round white knob and inched out the drawer in a smooth, stealthy motion. I could see from my first glance inside that the book was no longer there. There was a flame-coloured silk scarf rolled up like a small, soft nest in the corner, and a little silver tray scattered with a litter of black bobby pins. Toward the back of the drawer there was an opened package of licorice allsorts, a tiny opal ring, and a white bottle of pills.

The ring, I knew, was a gift from Linnie's father—he'd given it to her when they moved away from Australia when Linnie was still a little girl. She'd told me it would be mine in a few years, once my fingers had grown big enough for it to stay on my hand. I ignored it and took out the allsorts and unrolled the top of the package, wincing as it crinkled. It was not the book, but hidden candy was to be looked upon as a right. I scooped up a handful and dropped them into the pocket of my sundress. Then I replaced everything as it had been.

I chose a pink candy with a black centre and popped it into my mouth. Then I tiptoed to the doorway where I could hear Linnie still talking on the phone downstairs, the soft rising cadences of her voice offering me the promise of more time. My heart was beating very fast. I knew by the fact that the book had been moved since last night that it was something that Linnie did not want me to see. And I didn't want to be like Mim, one of those people who are always kept on the outside, no matter how many times they try to get you to let them in.

I turned my back on the open door and surveyed the room, which I thought of as Linnie's room, even though Garek slept there too. The den downstairs off the kitchen was my father's domain, filled with uninteresting books and anchored by a large desk stacked with papers.

It was as though I was my nighttime self, and I felt a thrill of danger in opening all of Linnie's drawers in turn. With each new drawer I gave a quick intake of breath, felt a nervous tingling somewhere below my stomach.

I found it in the bottom bureau drawer, beneath three folded sweaters. It was a small, thick book, bound in brown leather with creamy lined paper. The green fountain pen rested as a marker between the last written-on page and the blank pages that followed. The writing itself was a neat, tight cursive that I had never seen before. I frowned at the black lettering, peering at the round, even words. I was able to make out a line in which I saw my own name appear.

The emptiness goes on and on without you. And even Shay can't fill up what I've lost. Oh God, I miss you so much. Emma, Emma, Emma. It's like everything on earth has turned to stone.

I stared and swallowed, and the book slipped from

my fingers with a muted thump, a soft taupe sweater pillowing its return to the drawer. I had no idea why my name was there in the book beside a name that I had never heard. Emma. I closed my eyes the way I had sometimes seen Linnie do when she was trying to remember something, but I just saw the bright ghosts of the light trapped beneath my eyelids. I stood there until I moved my tongue and found it thick and alien, dried out like a sponge by my open-mouthed breathing. When I heard a sound I fumbled the book back into place, slamming the drawer a little in my haste.

SHE WAS STILL ON THE PHONE when I got downstairs, the receiver tucked behind her ear as she filed the fingernails of her left hand. I loved her emery board and the white block she used for making her nails shiny. She would never let me use them, though, or even do my nails for me, because she said I was too young to be vain and should enjoy the time I had. She said I would be worrying about my appearance soon enough.

She looked up at me and I mouthed, "I'm going to Mim's," and she nodded. I let myself out the front door and almost tripped off the step. The day was brighter than I expected, and as I squinted, my eyes took in the dirt gathered along the crease where the asphalt sloped toward the pavement like a long, dusty muffler warming the sidewalk. I saw, too, the power lines strung up between all the houses, the wires stretching in every direction, so thick and black I wondered how I had never noticed them.

In later years, I would think of reading the book as the moment when the first link was broken between who I once was and who I would grow up to be. It was as if a cord leading back to a simple kind of happiness had been severed, or maybe twisted, and in that walk over to Mim's I felt less like a girl and more like an ancient marionette pulled suddenly into the light, each part rattling stiff against the other with every creaking, tangled step.

Mim was the only girl I was friendly with, and she lived three houses down, in a white house with no front porch. I had heard Mrs. Gavranovic tell Linnie that Mim's only talent was making herself look good, the same gift Mim's mother had been born with. But I knew Mim also had a definite knack with a hula-hoop. I'd once watched her manoeuver one around and around her tiny waist while at the same time she sucked on a grape lollipop, grasping the stick with one hand after I screamed I'd tell if she didn't hold on to it. Mrs. Gavranovic had told me that when she was a little girl she had a next-door neighbour who choked on a lollipop. "He was too little to know to hold on to the sucker stick and the candy wound up lodged in his larynx." Mrs. Gavranovic's tongue slid to the corner of her mouth when she used medical language, and a savoury gleam appeared in her eyes, as though disaster was a roast lamb with garlic potatoes, or one of her own famous rhubarb pies, baked from the leafy red and green stalks that grew in her back yard.

"He stopped breathing and turned blue and would have died except that I yelled for his father who hung him upside down by his ankles and shook him and beat him on the back until the sucker came out."

It seemed obvious enough to me that this was the reason why foolhardy people were called suckers, but it did not clear up the issue of the word lollygagging and why Mrs. Gavranovic would use it so cheerfully to describe the way I wandered up and down our quiet block, stopping to investigate from a safe distance any new pieces of debris or unusual weeds that happened to crop up between my door and Mim's.

Mim's real name was Margaret Imogen Millar, but when she was a baby her godmother gave her a real gold bracelet with her initials on it, and her father and everyone else began calling her Mim—though her mother, in her fussy way, still called her Margaret. I was interested in Mim's godmother, not only because of the bracelet, which gleamed in the light like a piece of pirate's treasure, but because it seemed that Mim, too, had a second mother, one she had not seen since she was a baby, when her godmother moved to Milwaukee.

There were three small steps leading up to the front door, and this is where I found Mim, wearing a rose-coloured skirt and sweater set. Linnie said that Mrs. Millar dressed her like a teenager instead of a little girl, but I thought that Mim's smart outfits were one of her redeeming qualities. She was sitting with her legs together, one hand resting over each knee, doing absolutely nothing. Holding up her fingers and wiggling them at me in greeting, she informed me that her nail polish was drying. Sticky-looking mauve polish coated the ends of each of her fingers in a perfect illustration of Linnie's idea of premature maturation.

I climbed the stairs to get a closer look. Linnie's attention to her nails never included this last and most intriguing of step of applying polish. It occurred to me that painted nails would be one way of hiding the dirt that always seemed to accumulate underneath.

"Did your mother let you do that?" I asked.

"She did it for me," said Mim, replacing her hands palm down on her knees. "She told me to stay still until it was dry."

"Isn't there anything you can do while you wait?" I asked. "You could read, maybe."

Mim wrinkled her nose. "That's no fun. And my fingers could get stuck to the pages. Anyways, my parents are going to buy me a radio for my birthday."

"That's nice."

Mim sucked in her cheeks and crossed her wrists. I knew she was about to say something disagreeable. "My mother said that your father went away again."

"Yes," I said. I was walking the wooden border of their small front garden, staring down at my feet.

"She says she feels sorry for your mother being left on her own so much."

I looked up. "She's not on her own. I'm there."

Mim slowly stretched out her legs and crossed her ankles. "But she has to look after you." Mim gave me a serene smile that almost made me lose my balance near the overgrown bush of bleeding hearts. She went on, "She doesn't have any friends."

"She does too," I said, my defence automatic.

"No, she doesn't." Her voice was flat and confident. "My mother thinks your mother is too proud to be friends with anyone. She said it's just a sin the way you've all been here for five years and your parents can't be bothered to be anything more than just barely civil to anyone except for crazy Mrs. Gavranovic."

"She's not crazy," I muttered. Mim sniffed and raised her eyebrows. Her range of expression was marvellous. She had developed a series of significant looks that were very successful in making her seem much older than nine.

"My mother said she'd be glad to take a casserole over and make—" said Mim, then paused before continuing, "make overtures, because she feels so sorry for the two of you, but she's worried your mother would be offended."

I frowned. As much as I tended to dislike Mim, I left each of our encounters feeling a little more on my guard, a little more prepared to deal with the rest of the world. Mim didn't understand me, and later on I realized that this would be the way with most people—this had been one of the lessons of our friendship. It was why I didn't want her to find out I was adopted, and why I didn't want to ask her if she knew who Emma was. She already had too many reasons for thinking she was better than me. I didn't want to add my complete ignorance about myself and my family to the list.

"We don't need any casseroles, thank you," I said.

"You don't know what you need," pronounced Mim.

I hopped off the garden border. Mim was right. The words of the book had disoriented me, and she wasn't providing the kind of distraction I was looking for. But I knew better than to instigate a fight.

"I'm going now," I said. "Maybe we can play when your nail polish is dry."

"Okay," said Mim. "You know, you're lucky I don't mind playing with you sometimes. My mother says that you're to be pitied. She says you and your mother are a pair of loners."

I blinked. "See you later."

So I headed back toward my own house, turning Mim's last words over in my mind and thinking that Linnie and I had something in common, at least, whatever secrets might exist between us.

LATER ON I WATCHED LINNIE IN THE KITCHEN, making a cup of tea. She was tall and slender with fine, tawny hair tied back in a ponytail. Pressing her left hand into the edge of the counter, she poured hot water from the old-fashioned tin kettle. I looked at her hands as they moved, at the clean, pink fingernails and the clear blue veins on the inside of her wrists.

Stirring her tea, she joined me at the round wooden table, and I noticed that she moved differently when she wore a long skirt, swaying her hips more. As she sat down I looked away, fingering the orange tassels of

the woven placemat, worried she might begin to sus-
pect my secret knowledge of the hidden book upstairs.
I couldn't remember now whether I had always exam-
ined her this closely. Even though it had only been a
few hours, it seemed as though I could barely remember
anything about our lives before the book, as though it
was a dream I had mostly forgotten, a haze compared
to the intensity of the life I was now living. I stared into
my bowl of sliced bananas and milk, sinking each piece
in turn with the back of my small silver spoon.

I looked at Linnie's foot under the table, the fine
bulge of ankle above the scuffed, fringed moccasins.
Their halo of leather strands, furled and weathered,
looked like a circle of broken teeth, with tufts of fraying
fuzz to mark the strands that had been torn away. The
foot startled me in its unfamiliarity, in the way I could
separate it from the rest of her and make it into somebody else's foot, a foot I didn't recognize or had never
even looked at before.

"What is it, darling?" asked Linnie. "What little treasure have you spotted down there?"

I found new pieces of treasure all the time. Once
it was an old metal shoehorn in the back yard, whose
purpose was still puzzling to me even after I learned its
name, and another time a much-prized bead of royal-

blue glass. More recently, a long, smooth cork stamped with a design of grapes, stuck beneath the bottom of the oven. The cork was spongy and compact and perfect for rolling down the length of the hallway.

"Nothing," I said. "There's nothing down there at all."

Linnie peered at me with her hand pressed to the side of her face.

"What's going to happen to us," she said, "if you insist on being a mystery?"

To which I had no answer, for, as far as I was concerned, it was Linnie, not me, who was suddenly a mystery.

BEGINNING THAT AFTERNOON, I began to time my mother's absences, dividing them into explained and unexplained. Groceries, dry cleaning, and other errands were all accounted for, and I usually accompanied Linnie anyway. In the house, she was often in the kitchen—cooking, listening to the small black-and-silver transistor radio tuned to the CBC. I liked watching her cook. Sitting on the freezer or on the wooden set of drawers that held the cutlery and the utensils, I competed with the hourly news, talking loudly to amuse her while my heels banged a rhythm on the side of whatever I was sitting on. But sometimes Linnie would leave the room without any explanation, slipping out in silence like a needle lifting off a record. It might have been something Linnie had always done, this soundless glide, but now it struck me with the force of a revelation.

At first I began by simply following her, trailing in her wake like an afternoon shadow, but then Linnie would turn and take my hand and come back into the living room or the kitchen as though she had never left. Once I turned to find her absent and discovered her a few minutes later at the messy desk in the back study, running her hands over the piles of paper. Another time, I located her in the garden, a pail, already half-full of weeds, hanging from the crook of her left elbow.

After a few days of this watchfulness, it became clear that I had already uncovered her usual habit when I'd seen her writing in the book before bed. I had not surprised her at it again, but each night I slid on my belly across the hardwood floor from my own room, feeling every bubble and flaw in the varnish through the thin cotton of my nightgown. Pausing before the faint patch of light coming from the doorway, I strained my ears until I heard what I gradually became certain was the sound of a pen scratching on paper. That knowledge established, I stopped following her but continued to monitor her from a distance, silently and patiently, and always with my fear beside me.

It never occurred to me to try reading the book the whole way through, though it wasn't a sense of guilt that stopped me. Everything in that house was part of my domain, and I had a proprietor's outlook on all of it. It was only Linnie's book that threatened things, that hinted at something outside our tiny world of three. And I didn't like seeing my name written inside it, as though I was somebody who could be summed up and talked about just like anybody else. So though I thought a lot about the book, and even more about its mysterious Emma, I left it alone, nervous of what else it might contain. But I was still determined to find out who Emma was, even if I had to go about it in a different way.

→

GAREK SOMETIMES CALLED LINNIE his Down-Under Dame, which I knew was a way of saying that she was Australian, but I liked to repeat Down Underwear after he said it until a fit of giggling stifled me or Linnie intervened. I always stopped when she asked me to because I liked hearing about Australia even more than I liked making the joke. It seemed wonderful to me that Linnie could have come all the way from the other side of the world.

Mostly what I knew about Australia was that it was very hot. Linnie said she had an uncle who died from the heat in the desert. He was a favourite of hers because he was an adventurer who travelled all over the continent and brought her back trinkets and, even more importantly, thrilling stories of his escapades. Her opal ring came from such a journey, from a place called Andamooka. When her uncle died he was trying to make his way across a southern desert.

"There were no roads," Linnie told me, "only dirt paths, and it's easy to lose your way because there are hardly any trees and the land goes on and on forever. My uncle ran into some Aborigines, who were kind to him and brought him to shelter, but he was already too dehydrated and he died on the way."

"Do you miss him?" I asked her once. I wondered if Linnie's uncle died in a tent, and if a medicine man tried to heal him with herbs and potions.

"I thought I did," she said. She was settling onto the couch, speaking in the low voice that she used in the early stages of a headache. I pulled the blinds closed with an unnecessary flourish and I saw her wince. She placed a light cotton handkerchief over her face. "That is, whenever I thought about him, I wished I could see him again." Linnie sighed, and the lower half of the handkerchief quivered with her exhalation. "I realize now that isn't the same thing as really missing someone."

I liked to find my way into Garek's study during the times when Linnie had a headache. The study was a small, close room in the corner of the house, made even smaller by rows of bookshelves lining one of the walls. Often, Garek would be staring at the wall of books, lips parted, one hand in his thatchy blonde hair, his fingers digging through the tangles like a pitchfork spearing hay. He always looked surprised to see me, which might have been because of his deep concentration, or because Linnie so rarely looked for him there, or maybe because his face was still so much like a boy's that it rumpled with every current of emotion.

"You startled me," he said this time, as I poked my head through the doorway. He smiled at me, his face relaxing as he pulled his hands away from his hair.

"You creep around so quietly, like a little hunter." He held out his hands and lifted me up onto his lap. I could smell the saltiness of his neck mixed with the clean bleach smell of his collar. I leaned my head against his chest and felt his muscles jump at my touch, like Linnie's hand when she cooked and a drop of hot oil leapt from the pan to her wrist. Then, just as quickly, he relaxed, cracking his knuckles as he joined his hands around my middle. I ran my fingers over the blonde hairs growing like wind-blown grass on his arms.

"I'm not hunting you," I said. I lifted up my hands to show him that I had no weapons, and Garek laughed. He had told me stories about how skilled hunters could track an animal for days, just by following a trail of broken branches, or prints in the snow. Sometimes even a stray feather, or the sound of water in the distance, would be enough to help them find their target.

"Well, even so," he said. "You're a model of stealth, like Mr. Hoover of the FBI."

"Mr. Vacuum Cleaner," I said, because this was another joke I always made, and I reached with my feet for the legs of the chair, the surface of which I could just barely brush with my two big toes. Garek called it a captain's chair. It was made of wood and had little wheels on the bottom. I got Garek to roll us over to the big map of Canada that he had hanging on the wall.

There was a constellation of red and white push pins on the map, each marking what Garek called his "special places": towns and reservations he'd visited all over the country, but mostly bunched in a ragged arc sweeping up and left from the lonely yellow tack marking the capital with our house in it. The five points of our city's circled star were just visible around the metal shaft of the pin, unlike the dots marking the other places, which were all so small that the pins wiped them out. Garek knew most of the map by heart.

"This is Manitou Mounds," he said, pointing, "here on the Rainy River." He knew I liked the map, and I knew even then that he wanted me to love its swaths of white and blue and its delicate black script, and especially the northern expanse, where the clumps of land huddled together like pieces of a puzzle. He always picked names that shot thrills across the ridge of my shoulders and sent my thoughts whirling outward into the world, to the kinds of places where everything might be different and magical.

"Have you been there?" I asked. He nodded.

"Of course." He pointed to another pin, one of several circling the top of Lake Superior. "See that white thumbtack? That means I've been there." He let go of me with one hand to scratch his head just above his ear. "The red ones are places I'm in charge of but haven't visited yet."

Garek wheeled us back around to his desk. "The greatest thing about my job," he said, "is getting to travel, and sometimes I get to go to places that most people will never see." Garek squeezed me and his breath tickled my ear. "One day you'll go places, too, Shay. You'll see and do things that little girls like you could never even have dreamed of fifty years ago."

Fifty years seemed like an impossibly long time since even five minutes could sometimes seem as long as an hour, like the times Linnie said, "Five more minutes!" when she called me in for dinner when I was playing with Mim. I don't know whether it was because I was hungry, or because Mim was so tiresome, but the intervals between Linnie's calls seemed to drag out forever.

"How many minutes are there in fifty years?" I asked.

"A lot," said Garek. "A ton."

IN THE DINING ROOM, by the antique china cabinet where she stored the medicine in the darkness behind the cups and saucers, Linnie was pouring cod-liver oil into a small silver spoon. Maybe my anxiety about Emma showed in my face, because Linnie was convinced I was coming down with something. She kept feeling my forehead with her cool, slender hand, her brow lowering with the weight of her concern.

"You're a hot little potato," she said, passing me the spoon with its glass-like golden bubble of oil. "What do you think about starting school a little bit late?"

Eyes closed, I swallowed the oil and said I thought that

would be fine. I had never been to school before, but my interest in it had dwindled with the start of my new obsession. I wanted to stay close to Linnie. Those few words I'd read about Emma occupied a strange place in my brain. The more I thought about it, the more I wondered whether I had sometimes heard her name before, long ago, carried on the breath of one of Linnie's long sighs, or whispered between my parents once I was supposed to be asleep. And whether or not this was true, it only made me more certain that Emma was somebody important. Some days I could think of nothing else, and I spent all my energy watching Linnie and coming up with different ideas about who Emma might be. At other times, the whole thing would slip away from me for a moment, but it was never really gone, like an old scab that kept coming off and hardening over, becoming a little more painful and familiar each time.

"I think I might be coming down with something, too," said Linnie. She stooped to bring my hand up to her forehead. "Do I feel feverish?" she asked. Her pale eyelashes fluttered as she held my wrist.

"Yes," I said, enjoying the warmth against my skin.

"Maybe it's just this Indian summer that's making me so hot," she said. "It's hard to get used to the heat again after there's already been a frost."

She decided then that I would stay home with her for

a month or two, or as long as it took for me to get back to my old self.

"It's not as though you're going to be missing anything you don't already know," she said, as she stroked my hair. "My smart little Shay."

→

I COULDN'T REMEMBER EXACTLY when the words in the books Garek read me began to make sense on the page. He taught me the letters and their sounds, and from time to time, we sounded out a word together. At first he thought that I had memorized the Curious George book we were reading, that I simply knew when to turn the pages, but after he pressed me to try it with a book I had never seen before and I still turned every page at exactly the right moment, he hugged me so tightly I had to yell for him to let me go. After that he made a ritual of bringing books home, usually on the way back from one of his trips. I noticed that the more time I spent reading Linnie's mother's old religious books from the downstairs bookcase, the more quickly he was guaranteed to bring me home something else.

When Garek returned from Fort Albany, he brought home a Nancy Drew book that he'd bought in Toronto.

He told me the cover made him think of me. I thought this was strange, since in the picture Nancy looked more grown up than me—and blonde besides—but when I asked he said it was because she looked curious and brave, poised as she was in the branches of a tree, looking over a fence toward a suspicious-looking rooftop.

I read the book outside in the hammock, holding it up with both hands to keep it between my face and the sun. Then, when my arms got tired, I wriggled over onto my side, my nose brushing against one of the facing pages. It was a much, much longer book than any I had read before. It was frustrating how long it took to finish even a short chapter, let alone keep my place with all the text swimming across the page. Garek read from it at night to bring me forward in the story so I wouldn't get discouraged.

My skirt felt gummy against my legs as I lay there, a prisoner of the humidity which lay like a sheet of cellophane over the yard. Every once in a while a fly buzzed loud in my ear and I yelled, annoyed, until I realized that each time I tried to swat one I set the hammock rocking, a hint of a welcome breeze skimming across my hot cheek.

What excited me most about the book was the idea of a girl being a detective. Nancy's reaction to mystery was not bewilderment and fear, as mine was. She set out to find answers to her questions, instead of making herself sick with worry. Even more impressive, she had good friends who would follow her into danger.

It was with Nancy as inspiration that I was listening outside my parents' door after my bedtime, trying to stay silent in the darkened hallway.

"I never know what you're thinking." Linnie's voice was so quiet I could barely hear it.

The floor creaked loudly on the other side of the door, and as I slid backwards toward the wall, I heard Garek say, "I'm not sure that's a bad thing." And then, after a pause and with a leaden sigh, "Nothing, it's nothing." I heard him take a step toward the closet and cough. "Have you ever heard the term pencil-pusher?"

I hadn't, but I wondered if he didn't really mean pedal-pushers, like the smart yellow pair owned by Mim and trimmed with drawstrings and bows where they ended just below her knees. I thought Linnie might correct him, but I didn't hear her response.

"I'm not helping anyone." Garek's voice was flat now. "I just do my little tours and write reports. And my reports all say the same thing because if they don't I'll never get promoted out of writing the damn things." I heard the swish and thud of a pair of belted pants hitting the floor.

"How do I know what's going on up there? It's so isolated. Living on James Bay is like squatting at the edge of the earth. You might as well fall in for all anybody cares. The trees wouldn't notice." Garek coughed again. "And there's very little accountability. In some cases, it's only me."

"Come here," said Linnie, and I could hear the bedsprings creak as they gave under Garek's weight. "What are you worried about? It's not as though the priests and nuns could even waste government money if they tried. There's nothing to spend it on up there." And then, "When are you going to get over your anti-religion crusade? Good people go to church, too, you know, including your wife."

There was silence for a moment, and then I heard Garek say, "You don't look well."

"I'm tired," replied Linnie. And then, "I'm fine."

"Are you sure?"

"I'm just lonely." She gave a low laugh. "I have a tendency to brood, you know." Then she said, with a breathy sigh, "I wish you didn't have to go away again so soon."

"Believe me, so do I."

Linnie was so quiet now that I had to strain my ears to hear, brushing the top of my head against the door frame and flexing my toes against the wooden floor like an athlete at the beginning of a race.

"And I'm worried about Shay. What if she gets sick? She's so quiet these days."

"She's fine. She's healthy." And then, "She's not Emma."

"No," said Linnie, "she's not."

When I got back to my room, I slipped back into bed and lay there with the light on, my shoulders flat and rigid against the flannel sheet. I drummed my fingers on the mattress as though I could press my uneasiness into its mass of springs and foam, letting it soak in and sink to the bottom. I felt comforted by the tautness of my freshly made bed and the way it forced me to keep still. I was sealed in, a letter within an envelope, ready to be delivered. Complete. Complete except for my utter lack of knowledge about the person closest to me in the world.

With my restlessness hampered by the sheets, my fingers and toes kept up a manic rhythm, twitching in time to my anxious thoughts. It was clear that Emma, whoever she was, was as important to Linnie as I was, or maybe even more so. And she was a secret, which meant that she had to do with something special, or bad, or hurtful to me. Maybe a sickly younger sister with whom Linnie had had a falling out, a terrible fight that drove her away forever. Linnie claimed to be an only child but that might be a lie. I saw at once that everything I had ever been told might be untrue. Emma might even have been an adopted girl Linnie and Garek had decided to return, someone who had been such a disappointment that she had to be sent back to where she came from. Maybe I was her replacement, the new hope for the family.

I was frightened by this thought, but also stimulated. It was as though I was being shaken awake from such a deep sleep that there might be no end to how much more I might see and come alive to. Sleep now seemed like an enemy trying to keep me on the outside of Linnie and Garek's secrets, as pacified and ignorant as any other child. "I will never sleep again," I thought.

I repeated that sentence out loud into the darkness, and I liked the resolution that flowed through me as I said the words. But at some point my eyelids began to flutter, and when I closed my eyes completely, I could see all of the possible Emmas lined up, an endless chain of sick girls and women, feverish and coughing as they lured me toward oblivion.

IT TURNED INTO THE HOTTEST INDIAN SUMMER that anyone could remember. Whenever she walked past our house, Mrs. Gavranovic complained that she would rather have

the rheumatoid than the blasted hellfire heat that was trying to cook her into an early grave. Garek was only ever to
be found in his shirt sleeves, even at the beginning of the
day on his way to work. At these times, his jacket seemed
like another victim of the heat, limp and deflated where it
lay folded over his arm. Linnie was quieter than usual on
the hot days. She bathed our wrists in ice water, and for a
time our slight exhalations of pleasure and relief became
our only conversation.

Mrs. Gavranovic's house became an increasingly ap-
pealing afternoon destination for me as October wore
on. As Linnie's headaches became more frequent, she
spent more of every day sleeping them off on the sofa. I
thought, too, that Mrs. Gavranovic might know something
of my mother's secrets, and that given the right moment
she could be persuaded to tell me. I had been studying
Nancy Drew's techniques for solving mysteries and was
planning situations where I could put them to use.

Mrs. Gavranovic lived in an old house that stayed
cool no matter what the temperature. It had high ceilings
and smooth, creaking floorboards, and dark, heavy furniture shiny with polish. Mrs. Gavranovic often praised
the builders of her house and said that insulation was the
key to everything.

"God have mercy on their souls," she said, and her

voice warmed with true affection for the men who must have long since died but who had earned her lasting goodwill with their dedication to fine workmanship.

I arrived on her doorstep straight after lunch, clutching a tin of Linnie's sponge cake.

"You're getting very dark in all this sun we're having, aren't you?" she said when she saw me, shading her eyes against the full afternoon light.

She took the tin from me as I was drawing my clean loafers over the flat edge of the curlicued iron bootscraper. She clucked as she opened it, her nose dipping almost right down to the white wax paper lining the can.

"It smells good," she judged, "but it's going to be dry."

I followed her into the kitchen, and she passed me a tray of her own baked dainties as she jabbed at my mother's golden cake with one round, wrinkled finger.

"She tries," she said. Mrs. Gavranovic could infuse any remark with her own flavour of buoyant melancholy, each word graced with its own sigh.

"Lord knows she tries, the poor woman. And it's not bad cake, no." She shook her head again and ushered me into the living room. "No, I'll never say it's bad, but it's not good either, if you know what I mean."

She closed the door behind me, and as I did know what she meant, I allowed myself a moment of pleasure before giving in to a mild feeling of dutiful indignation, stuffing a square of iced carrot cake into my mouth before it could fully take hold.

"Set that cake on the table," she instructed me. I did so and perched opposite her on a pink upholstered loveseat. Mrs. Gavranovic poured me a cup of weak tea then set the pot back down to steep.

"So how is she?" she asked. Mrs. Gavranovic already had an exhaustive knowledge of Linnie's headaches and spells of fatigue, and I only hoped she wasn't about to recommend another of her grandmother's home remedies.

"She's okay," I said, and I was stricken again with the pulse-racing nervousness that came over me whenever I considered asking about Emma. "She's resting this afternoon." I sipped my tea and tried not to kick my feet. Mrs. Gavranovic filled her own cup and drank it at once.

"Rest is life's greatest physician," she said. "It's a good thing you have someplace to come to, child, to help your mother keep her strength up."

"Yes," I said. "That is a good thing." Mrs. Gavranovic stood up to begin clearing the tea things, and I saw a landslide of crumbs tumble down her poppy-patterned apron to the floor.

"She's a child herself, that one," she said, with a trace of indulgence, and I saw my opportunity.

"Especially after Emma," I ventured, busying myself with leaning forward and replacing my empty teacup in its saucer.

"Oh Lord, yes," said Mrs. Gavranovic without a pause. She had turned from me to carry the tea tray out to the kitchen. "Or so I imagine. That kind of thing is hard on the best of us."

I heard the wet rattle and clink of the cups and saucers in the sink, then Mrs. Gavranovic calling out, "My own nephew divorced his wife over something like that. She blamed him for losing Sarah, though it was hardly his fault, the poor man. She had the leukemia."

Mrs. Gavranovic reappeared, drying her hands on the skirt of her apron.

"I don't hold with divorce in general," she told me, "but I'm not like those that say it shouldn't be allowed."

I nodded my head mechanically as she settled back into the gold-coloured rocker. It creaked and squeaked as it slid back along the floor. I said, "What's divorce?"

Mrs. Gavranovic let out a kind of hoot. "Well, isn't that just the most precious thing? Of course you don't know, doll, and why should you? When I was married I never let the word pass my lips inside my own house. Look, you just go on home and forget you ever heard it."

GOING HOME FROM MRS. GAVRANOVIC'S, I let my feet drag as my eyes logged the blankness of the concrete. I knew what leukemia was, or at least what it did, for I had heard it from Linnie's lips as she read the paper, murmured in the quiet and respectful tones reserved for tragedy. She had told me something of it, enough for me to catalogue it alongside the other death-dealing illnesses I had heard of, like smallpox, tuberculosis, and scarlet fever.

I couldn't remember when I had first learned of death itself, with its unfathomable stopping and its set of sorrows which came to a family as reliably as Christmas presents. But I do remember walking home from Mrs. Gavranovic's that day and becoming certain all at once that Emma was Linnie and Garek's adopted daughter, that she got sick and died, and that I was her replacement. And when I cried later in my room, I told myself that I was crying for Linnie and Garek, and for how sad they must have been when it happened.

I WOKE UP NERVOUS THE NEXT DAY, my hands stiff and tender as though they'd been clenched tight all night

long. I turned up at Mim's house and coaxed her over
to play in my yard. She said she might as well since she
was bored anyway. Mim's boredom was the backbone
of our friendship. It guaranteed a few hours in which
I could make Mim play at what I wanted with enough
grudging willingness for us to squeeze out a little fun.
Mim's only game was a version of House in which she
tiptoed around in imitation of her mother in high heels,
asking her husband—usually played handily by a tree
stump or large rock—how he liked his steak cooked. I
was the daughter she would nag and scold with gusto.
The sessions always ended with Mim sitting on the swing
as I kneeled in front of her and allowed her to play with
my hair.

At first this reward was enough to make me go
along with what I viewed as an otherwise boring game.
Mim's mother set Mim's blonde waves in smart clusters
of curls or into the mystery of French braids, two neat
plaits cresting the sides of her head like twin mountain
ranges. But our game usually ended with my hair in
some monstrous arrangement as I knelt unaware, my
cheeks flushed with the promise of beauty. One time
Mim backcombed my thick black hair so badly that it
took Linnie almost three hours to untangle it and she
put an indefinite ban on the game, or at least on Mim's

tenure as my personal stylist.

"Let's play Saints," I suggested, once we were en-closed within the haven of my back yard. Saints was one of my games, fuelled by the collection of children's religious books on the second shelf of the downstairs bookcase. I was fascinated by the saints. I had a morbid affection for the awful pain of the martyrs and an envy of their specialness. I had read the books so often that their stories were more familiar to me than my own. And when we played the game, I had the power of making something happen. I could make Mim interested enough in the story to follow my direction in acting it out, for she had a hankering to be an actress.

The key was in suggesting the kind of story that I knew would appeal to her: anything with a young fe-male heroine who suffered terribly, which was the kind of story I preferred, anyway. There were lots of saints like that—St. Agnes, St. Cecilia, St. Felicity—so it wasn't hard. St. Agatha was a particular favourite. Her tribula-tions included having her breasts hacked off and dying in a spectacular earthquake sent by God to spare her further torture.

Mim put in a couple of hours as a lacklustre St. Catherine of Alexandria, barely holding back her yawns when, with God's help, the spiked wheel she was about to be tortured on was destroyed at her touch.

"What's the point of these stories?" she said. "They always end up dying in the end, anyway."

She squinted into the sun, her head still thrown back in the pose of a defiant martyr. I frowned at her. It was true that God only seemed to save somebody so many times and then he just let them die. Delivering someone from torture only to allow them to be beheaded was a puzzling kind of divine intervention.

I leaned back against the oak tree and shrugged.

"I don't know." Mim was now sitting carefully on the side of the hammock. "Do you want to do St. Cecilia?" I asked.

Mim stretched her arms and pushed her blonde curls behind her ears. "You're weird, you know that?" She stood up and brushed her hands over the skirt of her dress. "This is boring," she said. "I'm going home."

"But I'm having fun," I said, which was a lie, but I didn't want her to go.

Mim shrugged. "Well, I'm not. And even if I was, I need to get home anyways. My mother says I spend too much time hanging out with Aussies and savages."

Garek often told me not to be a savage when I played with my food before eating it, like making train tracks across the mashed potatoes with my fork, or piling peas and carrots into a pyramid. But his voice was always play-ful.

"What's an Aussie?" I said.

"Your mother," said Mim. She smirked. "It means she comes from Australia and is descended from a bunch of thieves and murderers." Mim laughed, then turned her back on me and stalked out.

"I hate you," I said, after she left. I pulled out three flowers from the garden, crushed them, and buried them in the dirt near the elm tree.

Then I spent the rest of the afternoon on the grass, reading more stories of the saints as the sun darkened my shoulders and dazzled my eyes. When I finally went inside it was as though I was blinded, everything in the house changed to shadows and angles.

THE DAY OF THE STORM began bright and searing. Even the breeze was hot and brought no relief, only funnels of blowing, gritty sand. It felt like the earth was trying to burn off its old skin and shed it like a winter coat, and the heat coming off the asphalt made the road look shimmering and wet in the distance. I sat barefoot on our square patch of front lawn, stretching each of my feet in turn to feel the burn of the sun-baked side-walk.

As I drew back my left heel, I felt a tickling on my other ankle. A small black ant was making a trek across the top of my foot. I drew in my breath quickly and leaned forward, my hands gripping at the grass, and, with an effort, steadied my leg, which had already begun twitching.

Linnie had explained that insects were actually fascinating creatures. The week before, she'd released a brown-legged spider we'd found on the calico cookie jar. She told me about giant spiders and about anthills in Australia that were taller than Garek. "Isn't that incredible?" she said. "Imagine something as tiny as a bug building something bigger than a man."

She had also told me about koalas and kookaburras and wombats. But more than all of those I liked the stories of the kangaroos that kept their babies in a pocket on their stomach.

The ant seemed to be having doubts about the sturdiness of its mountain, making for the fastest way down off my foot, so I put out a finger directly in its path. When it stepped on with as much apparent trust as if I were a tree or a rock or any other part of the scenery, I just managed to keep myself from singing out in triumph.

"Shay! Come inside, please. Lunch is ready!"

I made a barely audible noise in my throat. I turned

my hands over and over, letting the ant run from one to the other. I was entranced by its tiny efficiency, by its almost imperceptible body that was a model of action. Its legs moving across my skin tickled, and I bent my head to it, my nose down so far I thought there was a chance it might crawl inside. The ant was so precious and small. I felt as though I understood what it would be like to be a scientist, the kind of person who wanted to really see how the parts of the world worked.

"Shay!" called my mother again. She sounded impatient.

"I'm coming!" I said, keeping as still as possible. I felt like I always imagined I'd feel if I got up close to a horse or a pet of my own—as though animals would understand me, would understand how much I wanted to communicate with them. I tried to focus my thoughts into a beam heading straight for the ant.

"Shay!"

Hearing my name yelled in anger was so startling that I let my arm drop. The ant fell. I gave a yell and dropped to my knees, combing the grass with my fingers, furious at myself and at Linnie for interrupting me. I hoped I could find it again. I could feel bits of dirt becoming trapped beneath my fingernails as I shouted back that I was busy, that I was coming in a minute.

When I heard a shriek and the clanging of metal, I ran inside to the kitchen where Linnie was bent over the counter, a stack of plates in her hands and her hair hanging in her face. The big steel pot was overturned on the floor, and creamy leek soup, still steaming, ran over the floorboards in white waves, a milky sea spreading almost to the tips of my toes. Linnie was crying. I took a step backwards.

"I'm here," I said. "I'm sorry. There was this ant—"

"Please." Linnie's voice was thick as she turned to face me. "Don't." Her head moved from side to side then jerked toward the floor. "I spilled the soup," she said. I took a step closer and she laid the plates down on the counter, heaving a sigh that shook her chest and shoulders.

"I worry, you know," she said, wrapping her arms around her sides until her fingers hooked into the gaps at the back of her loosely crocheted blue sweater. "You didn't answer and I was worried." She hunched forward as though bracing herself against a downpour, but her lips were tremulous and pools of tears filming her eyes began to quiver and glint in the light. She let out a short, thin laugh, which frightened me, but I went to her anyway.

"I know," I said, "I'm sorry."

"My darling," she said, stroking my head harder than

I would have liked. "Don't ever leave me." I wasn't sure if she was speaking to me or not, because it sounded like the words from a song off one of Garek's records, but I promised I wouldn't. By the time we'd cleaned up the spilled soup, she'd called Mrs. Gavranovic and asked if she could send me over there for a while.

"I can feel one coming on," she said into the phone, as I stood on the stepstool to wring soup out of another dishcloth.

When she hung up, I asked her if I shouldn't stay instead. "I can bring you pills," I said. "Water. I can bring you anything you need."

Linnie shook her head. "I'm fine. I'll be fine."

AT MRS. GAVRANOVIC'S, I accepted the weak tea I was offered and wriggled into the pink loveseat until I could lean up against its back and feel the shaking of my body settle into stillness.

Mrs. Gavranovic hung up the telephone.

"That poor child," she said. "She's going to have a rest now, honey, so you're to stay here with me until the rain clears up, or she starts to feel a little better, whichever comes first."

The rain had come pelting down just as Mrs. Gavranovic closed the door behind me. I could see it now through the window, the drops hitting the sidewalk so hard they created a spray.

"Is she okay?" I said. I wanted to ask if Linnie was going to be angry at me forever, or, worse, if I had broken her beyond the hope of anyone's fixing. I twisted the skirt of my sundress between my fingers.

"She's at her wits' end, I think," said Mrs. Gavranovic with both relish and sympathy, "and it's not your fault, child, so don't look so terrified." A sigh escaped her as she settled down onto the chesterfield, the deep folds of her cheeks trembling with the movement. "There's a lot of pain that woman has seen."

I thought of all the pain that Linnie might feel if something were to happen to me and wondered if it would be more than all the pain I seemed to be causing her now. I laid one hand on my chest where I thought I felt a pang.

"Did you ever meet Emma?" I asked Mrs. Gavranovic. I wanted so badly to know about Emma and at the same time was afraid to find out. I watched Mrs. Gavranovic's face move among different expressions of emphasis. Her ruddy cheeks seemed to lengthen as she pursed her lips and shook her head, folding her arms across her large bosom.

"Lord, no, child. She died before they came here.

That's *why* they came here, it seems to me. Painful memories and all that."

She sniffed and rubbed her nose. "You're right smart to see that that's what's at the root of all this. Though I don't believe in leaving the past behind, no matter how painful. If you don't have your memories, what do you have? I pray to the Lord every night that I don't go senile. It's a terrible burden on the family, terrible."

Mrs. Gavranovic gave a pointed look toward the top of the piano where framed photographs of her grown children were lined up along a white lace runner, a permanent audience to their mother's sermons. Then she gestured around the room with her right hand.

"I wouldn't want to move away from here, either, where Mr. Gavranovic brought me home as a bride. Sometimes I almost expect to see him coming straight down the stairs to dinner, with his hands on his big belly, complaining of his hunger as he did until the day he died."

We both looked toward the empty staircase. I wondered what Mr. Gavranovic had thought of the ruffled banister decoration which ran up the length of the handrail, criss-crossing between each of the posts, magenta ribbons spilling from its frills of eyelet lace.

"But to tell the truth," continued Mrs. Gavranovic, "I met your mother on the first day they arrived and she said your father's work transferred him here. But why would the Department of Indian Affairs send him away from Winnipeg when there are so many more Indians there than here?"

Mrs. Gavranovic reached toward the toothpicks in their miniature brown-and-cream ceramic jug on the tea tray. She rolled one back and forth between her broad fingers and nodded.

"So, you see, I knew that wasn't the whole story. This place already has so many government men. Your poor mother told me the whole story before long. I could see plain enough she was in pain and needed help, Lord love her. Especially when I saw you, child, the poor baby you were then." She shook her head even as she tilted it back, operating the toothpick with a precise in-and-out motion. Her words were difficult to make out as she drew back her lips. "They're very adventurous people, your parents," she said, "except when it comes to what I call facing up to the cards that God has seen fit to deal them. I don't support the way they've tried to keep it all buried down."

"I thought God didn't like cards," I said.

"Right you are, child. A figure of speech," said Mrs. Gavranovic.

"And I thought Indians lived in the forest," I said.

Mrs. Gavranovic reached out to place the used

toothpick onto the tray. She rubbed her thighs a little and looked at me for a long time.

"Well," she said, with a curious precision, "some of them do, child. And some of them live in those schools that your daddy takes them to, so they can learn how to be clean and live properly and worship the Lord."

I nodded. She frowned.

"You're a good girl, Shay," she said at length.

"Thank you."

Mrs. Gavranovic let out a long breath. She smiled at me, and I could see a pink spot on her tooth from where she had made her gums bleed a little. "I think you'll turn out just fine in spite of everything."

I stared. "Um, thank you."

Mrs. Gavranovic beamed and helped herself to another piece of shortbread. "Think nothing of it, child. I'm not one of those that say what's bred in the bone can't be worked out by the Lord."

"Oh," I said. I looked down at my lap, where cookie and cake crumbs had pooled in the creases of my dress. "That's good," I said.

"Well," said Mrs. Gavranovic.

She cocked her head to the side.

"You know, I did see a picture of the child, once, with some coaxing. A well-looking little girl in the photo, sure enough, but dead within the month of it being taken, if you can believe it. The eeriest thing. I have a photo of Mr. Gavranovic just the same, all done up in his Sunday finest the week before his poor heart gave out." Mrs. Gavranovic's bottom lip trembled. "It gave me such a strange prickling on the spine, let me tell you. Even more than the photograph I had taken of him in his casket."

That photo of Mr. Gavranovic hung in the kitchen, beside Mrs. Gavranovic's wall-mounted spice rack. She said she liked to keep it near where she cooked as a reminder of the dangers of gluttony.

"Even more than that," she went on, "the blessed child looked just like your mother, the spitting image. Like a little doll." Mrs. Gavranovic sighed. "And the most precious little dress, all white lace and ruffles. Yes, a doll."

"That's funny," I said. I had pictured Emma looking just like me, only a little taller and prettier, with curly black hair instead of straight.

Mrs. Gavranovic gave me an odd look as she stood up to refill the teapot, huffing a little against the arm of the chesterfield.

"It's not what I'd call funny, child. It must give them pain night and day." She shuffled off into the kitchen, one hand on the small of her back.

I looked at the remnants of treats on the tray, and the beige droplets of tea on my saucer.

"But Mummy and Daddy weren't able to have children of their own," I said. "That's why they got me."

Mrs. Gavranovic popped her head out of the kitchen.

"Didn't your mother explain all this when she told you?"

I shook my head.

"Your mother got so sick when she had Emma that the doctor told her not to have any more babies of her own."

MOSTLY WHAT I THOUGHT ABOUT AT FIRST was how Linnie had lied to me. Being angry was braver than being sad, and when I could feel myself wavering, I only had to think, "She lied to me," until I was steadied. I slipped out Mrs. Gavranovic's gate and ran all the way to the end of the street and back. I saw the woman from the pink house stare at me when I passed her for the second time. When the stitch in my side became too painful to keep going and my breath started coming in gasps, I dashed through our gate and into the yard, collapsing onto the seat of the wooden swing.

My feet traced furrows in the dirt where I dragged them beneath me as I swung. I wanted to get off and go inside, but there was something comforting in the twisted surface of the rope, its rubbed heat tingling against my palms.

I squinted until my feet became a blur, a fast streak of white sock and brown loafer transforming into a vague smear above the darker earth I had overturned. I tried holding my breath for ten complete swings back and forth, but the exertion of pumping my legs caused me to let it all out in a burst, a rupture of gasping.

LOOKING BACK, I THINK I TOOK IT WELL, in the way that soldiers or refugees are said to take things well. Or the families of the dead. They are too bewildered or too drawn out from worry or too plain desolated to have any outward reaction to catastrophe. I had a sense of disbelief that prevented violent emotion, as well as a fascinated pleasure in my own numbness, like the way I would scratch and poke at my leg after sitting on it too long, until in time it gave way to pins-and-needles pain as the blood returned.

When the shock of the conversation with Mrs. Gavranovic at last began to wear off, I felt as though I had wandered into a fog, like the day Linnie and I took a walk in the early morning and we saw the mist rising off the ground. We could not see the fog while we were in it, but it hid everything before us, and when I looked back, it was covering the way that we had just come. I felt like I did then, with a portion of awe but also with the fear I would have felt if Linnie were not with me. I decided I was going to do whatever I could to help her love me as much as she had loved Emma.

IT WAS JUST LIKE PLAYING any other game at first. I was pretending to be somebody else, somebody I really wanted to be, like one of the martyrs. Only instead of being someone who was close to God I was going to be somebody who was close to Linnie. The only problem was that I knew very little about the person I was trying to be. The more time I spent thinking about her, the more that I began to see Emma as a perfect girl, a kind of saint or angel.

I was reading another book of saints before bed now, a leather-bound one with smaller print and fewer pictures. Linnie told me it was very old, from the time when her mother was a little girl. I already knew most of the female saints from the little picture books, so I'd decided to begin with the men. St. Alexius was my new favourite. He left home after his rich parents forced him into marriage, then returned as a pious beggar to live under their stairs. The remarkable thing about St. Alexius was that his own parents did not recognize him, never once in seventeen years, until he eventually died and was revealed by a note, a letter he had pinned on himself telling them everything.

WHEN GAREK CAME HOME AGAIN, Linnie's mood improved, although her head was still hurting more often than before. Instead of banishing me outside after lunch, she allowed me to keep her company as she worked through the tower of dirty dishes that had risen during his absence. I watched as she scoured off the scaly pieces of orange, the fluffy white mould that looked as soft as a cloud, and the liquid green seaweedy bits that she said used to be spinach. Tying a red bandana around her head, she tackled the chores with a rosy-cheeked enthusiasm, singing a little as she worked. She was pinning the violet-patterned pillow slips onto the backyard clothesline when she started on one of my favourite songs, about hammering in the morning and in the evening, and her face became open and loose. We laughed together until my stomach hurt when she pretended the clothes peg was a nail and she hammered it with her fist until the line wavered and jumped like a skipping rope and the laundry flapped like big white elephant ears.

She even agreed to take me shopping, once I'd
promised I wouldn't wander off and get lost or cling to
her elbow or complain of being bored, none of which
were unusual occurrences when I accompanied her to
the Bay downtown. Linnie was more indulgent with me
now that her headaches had come back, and at the same
time more distracted. She listened when I spoke to her,
but sometimes she seemed to be looking past me. She
hummed to herself as we walked and when she reached
for my hand I let her take it.

The women's clothing department was a strange,
colourful forest to me, each rotating rack bright with
its fabric foliage: silks, wools, and cottons, each to be
touched, compulsively, in turn.

A woman in a drooping blue hat scrutinized us as
we passed by. "Why is everybody staring?" I asked. I had
forgotten how much I hated the feeling of being looked
at everywhere we went. I kept close to Linnie's side,
thinking that the world outside of our house was more
exhausting than I remembered.

"Because we're so beautiful," said Linnie.

But I knew this wasn't true because I had heard Linnie described as beautiful and I looked nothing like her.

Linnie wound her way through the display racks,
pausing only a moment at each before breezing past.

When she headed toward the escalators without even having taken anything off the rack, I grabbed her hand and urged her to come with me to the children's department, which beckoned off to the left with its brightly coloured prints.

"I'm coming," she said. "Don't pull. I understand now why you wanted to be part of this expedition." We passed between two racks of blue-and-white sailor dresses.

"I don't think you need anything new just yet," she said. "Maybe in the fall."

I led her around some smooth-faced mannequins in fruit-coloured bathing suits and paused on the opposite side of their sleek yellow and orange backsides. Linnie looked around. A stray piece of straw-coloured hair had slipped from the loose knot at the back of her neck, and she twirled it in her left hand, chewing on the end in an absent way. Finally, I saw a rack of white dresses, including one with a lace skirt, just as flouncy and ruffled as Emma's dress in the photograph Mrs. Gavranovic had described. Its gathered folds gave me a tightness at the back of my throat, made me ache to be the kind of girl who would wear such a dress as a matter of course.

"Can I have it?" I said, and though such a demand

would normally result in a scolding, Linnie just shook her head.

"I really, really like it," I said. "I've never had a white dress."

Linnie's voice sounded bright when she said, "I have one at home for you already."

AT THE HOUSE, SHE MADE ME WAIT in my room, and I heard rustlings and muffled knockings from her closet. She came into my room a minute later, a white dress floating over her arm. It brought with it a mingled smell of cedar and roses. Sitting on the edge of my bed, she laid it down on the quilt between us.

"This is for you," she said, as I took in the fine eyelet lace at the seams and the glossy pink ribbons brightening the shoulders. There was a kind of ruffled smocking across the chest, with pink stitching in the form of tiny embroidered roses.

"Oh," I said, and Linnie smiled at me. I reached out my hand but stopped short of touching the clean white spread of the three-tiered skirt. I looked for signs that the dress had been worn, but there were none that I could see. Linnie kept her eyes on the dress and cleared her throat quietly.

"My mother made it, you know." She fingered the

hem, which was smooth with white ribbon.

"Really?" I couldn't picture anyone as cross as Mrs. Almead making anything so delicate and lovely. I had always imagined that she didn't like young people, and kept her windows and drapes closed against the sounds of children at her door or playing in the street.

"Yes, really." A sigh escaped her lips, so light it was musical.

"Who did she make it for?" I asked.

Linnie glanced at me for a moment, then looked away and circled the edge of one puffed sleeve with a pale index finger. I could now see that another matching pink ribbon, a half-width of the piece running around the shoulders, was woven into the lace edging and sewn into a delicate bow.

"For me," she said at last. "She made it for me. It's kept rather well, hasn't it? She could never do something like this now." Linnie paused. "Her arthritis is too bad." Her eyelids fluttered at me as her face turned almost coy.

"Do you like it?" she asked.

"I love it."

I had never had a dress as nice as this before, had only seen such things sometimes on Mim. We stood up and Linnie held it up before me by its shoulders and we could both see that it would fit. She was smiling and biting her lip, and I hugged her around the waist, the dress hanging over my arm.

"It's the best present ever," I said.

With Linnie's help, I put the dress on right away, and we ran downstairs together for what Linnie said was going to be our very own garden party. As we passed Garek's study on our way to the kitchen, he came to the doorway and hailed us.

"Where are you off to in such a hurry?" he asked. Garek's brown shirt was untucked and baggy around his waist, and he had untied his tie, which trailed down the sides of his chest like a scarf. He looked at me, and his hand began tugging at his earlobe.

"That's a pretty dress," he said, his voice flat. I knew from the way he said it that he had seen it before and that the dress was Emma's, no matter what Linnie said. I felt a tingling spread up and down my back and I hugged myself to keep from saying anything. Garek kept his eyes on Linnie.

"Isn't it?" she said, and after a moment, he nodded.

I twirled around, billowing the skirt, and when I stopped, he ruffled my hair.

"I'll join you," he said, and I ran ahead of them outside, into the long summer evening, feeling as light as the pink sash fluttering in my wake.

—

WE WERE SITTING IN THE NEGLECTED GARDEN, stretched out on the wicker Muskoka chairs. The grass had grown almost as long as the dandelions sprouting up between the pansies. I asked Linnie if she wanted my help with weeding, but she just shook her head, turning away from me without opening her eyes, drawing her straw hat a little farther down her forehead. Linnie was spending half her time giving me her undivided attention and the other half ignoring me completely, lost in reveries or maybe just brought low by the headaches.

A crow landed on one of the cucumber stakes, its tail feathers scraping the largest heart-shaped leaf. It took screeching to the air before either of us could raise an arm to shoo it, and Linnie watched it fly away, her hands resting on the top of her hat. She told me she remembered a scarecrow that used to stand in the field behind her parents' house in Australia. It was the first thing she had said in over an hour, and I felt as though the balloon being squeezed inside my stomach might finally begin to deflate. I turned to face her, reassured by how the alarming stillness of her face, which I had been sneaking glances at all afternoon, relaxed into familiar expressions as she spoke.

"He had a knit toque on, although I thought it was just a big sock until after I spent my first winter in Canada."

I watched her wiggle her toes, then bring her knees

up to her chest, wrapping her arms tight around them. "And he had a purple blazer and an orange scarf and the most crooked and sympathetic smile scrawled onto a pie-plate head. I even went to say goodbye to him the day before we moved."

I liked stories about when Linnie was a little girl and told her so. Her eyes were fixed on a spot near one of the top branches of the neighbour's elm tree, right where we'd last seen the crow's springy black form.

"I lost everything," she said.

"What?" I asked. I thought she must be able to hear my feet as they tensed against the wicker of the chair.

"When I left Australia," said Linnie, gesturing wide with her arms. "My friends, my world, everything." She reached for the glass of iced tea that had long since grown warm and watery. Then she stretched and said, "At the time, I felt as awful as if I'd been taken away from my own parents." Her gaze faltered, and she cleared her throat, returning the empty glass to the white iron table between us.

"Of course, they came with me," she said. "We all came to Canada together. But seeing them in another place made them feel strange to me, as though they were different people. More tired and worried." She shrugged. "But I think now that maybe they were always that way, and it was me who changed. Seeing the world against a different background changed everything for me."

"Is that why you wanted to leave?"

"Leave Winnipeg?" She sighed. After a long time, she said, "Yes, I guess so. I wanted another kind of change in scenery. Although there are always reasons to leave."

Something about the way she spoke made me realize that while it seemed as though people going places was the way of the world, everything moving ahead in time, it could all just as easily be turned around. It might be that really everybody was always leaving, that partings and separations were closer to the heart of things. I didn't like that idea at all.

I had managed to wear the white dress for so many days in a row that it was starting to get soiled and dingy. Its satin edges and lace trim had become stained like winter's shrinking leftovers, the dirt-topped frostings of snow left to line the sidewalks in early April. Linnie had said something about putting it in the wash that morning, but the rest of the dirty clothes were still piled in a heap around the overflowing hamper in the bathroom.

Once Linnie's silence had shaded into a less worrisome sleep, I tiptoed from my chair and onto the overgrown lawn. I watched as my feet trampled patches of grass, hundreds of long, cooling blades bent and cross-

ing like a woven mat. I noticed that at least the ruffled
smocking at the top of my dress was still free of spots,
and I hoped that its original owner, if she could see me,
wouldn't mind that I was wearing it.

"O dear, departed Emma," I thought, careful not to
mouth the words, "show me the way into your soul!"

It occurred to me that this kind of prayer had gone
badly for me before. I had once asked God to tell me what
to do and then became confused trying to distinguish between my own sinful impulses and the holy ones He was
sending. But I thought an angel might be different, might
even take the time to make a personal appearance, as they
always seemed to in the Bible. And I'd decided that little
girls like Emma, when they died, always became angels.

"Let me see you!" I spoke aloud, spreading my arms
wide, and adding, "I beg you."

I didn't fully expect to see her, but goosebumps
tingled over my arms and legs. Not only would I be able
to find out how to be like her, but she would be able to
tell me everything: why she died, why Linnie was so sad,
and why I felt so alone. And maybe even which of the
saints ought to be my favourite. She might know some
of them, after all.

"Appear before me!" I said, louder.

"Don't talk to God that way," said Linnie without

opening her eyes. "Go inside and be quiet, please."

So I went inside and tried to conduct my séance in the bathroom, hoping Emma wouldn't be picky about the location. Turning off the lights, I left the door open a crack so only a glimmer of light filtered through, creating an eerie semi-darkness and throwing a broad shadow across my face. With my voice at a whisper and my face in a solemn attitude of prayer, I pleaded with Emma to show herself. But no matter how suddenly I snapped open my eyes, I was still the only one standing before the mirror, and I could detect no trace of any fleeing ghostly presence, only the foolish racing of my own heart.

THE NEXT AFTERNOON MY MIND turned back to the book. I was just about to go inside to try and steal another look when Mim swung through the wooden gate to the back yard.

"What are you doing?" she said. She looked cross and ready to find fault. We hadn't spoken since our fight.

"Nothing," I said, and though she wrinkled her nose and frowned at me, the truth of my answer was so obvious that it gave her nothing to argue with.

She remained at the edge of the rock garden, her lips in a pout.

"I'm bored," she said, her pale chin jutting up.

I stood. "Let's play Rope Face," I suggested, and she agreed.

Rope Face was a game we had invented together one afternoon the previous summer, after Garek hung the hammock between the oak and an ailing elm, the only two trees in the yard. It consisted of one person lying face down on the hammock, her face pressed into its cross-knit fibres. The other person lay on her back on the ground underneath and laughed until her sides hurt at the way the rope twisted and contorted the other's face.

"I'll go first," I said, heading toward the trees at a run, but Mim hung back.

"I don't want to get my clothes dirty on the grass," she said. Her pink gingham skirt and white blouse were crisp with Mrs. Millar's bleach and precision ironing.

"I'll go and get a blanket," I said, thinking that while I was at it I would check on the book.

"Your dress is already dirty," said Mim. She was looking at me with unusual interest, taking in the lace and the ribbons. "You look funny wearing that," she said. She giggled.

"Why?"

Mim shrugged and scratched her nose, freckled in spite of Mrs. Millar's strict sunhat regimen. "You just look funny all dressed up," she said. "I guess that's why your mother doesn't take you to church with her. Are you going to go get that blanket? This is boring."

"No, it's not," I said. I suddenly hated the sight of Mim's prissy outfit and pouty face. "You're boring."

It was a new kind of remark from me and it seemed to strike a rare nerve somewhere deep within Mim's otherwise robust ego.

"No, you're boring!" she said, never wasting energy on being defensive when she could be the aggressor. "How dare you say that?"

I shrugged, and Mim's face got red.

"You're the most boring girl I've ever met," she said, "and everyone thinks you're weird-looking and your father doesn't really love you or he wouldn't go away so much and your mother is a head case who doesn't know how to take care of a man and if she doesn't take better care of your garden my mother is going to complain to the Neighbourhood Association and then you'll all have to move really far away and then you won't have any friends at all, not even me!"

Her lips were trembling and I thought that I had never seen her so furious or so vulnerable in her anger. But instead of feeling wounded, I was mad and annoyed. I stepped forward, and reaching up, I slapped her hard in the face.

Mim screamed and tears started spilling down her

flushed cheeks. I took a step backwards. She touched a
hand to her face, her eyes narrowing into pinholes of
rage.

"I hate you," she said. "I hope your house burns
down."

"I hope your hair burns off."

"You wish," she said, her mouth in a sneer as she
tossed her curls.

"Yeah, I do." I crossed my arms and smirked until
Mim's face crumpled.

As she ran off toward her own house, I yelled, "I
hate you, too!"

MIM'S MOTHER SHOWED UP right after lunch. Linnie was
dozing in the chair when the doorbell rang, her mystery
novel lying closed in her lap. When she opened the door
Mrs. Millar began speaking at once.

"I suppose you know why I'm here," she said, em-
phasizing every second syllable. Her hair, an upturned
blonde bob, shook with each beat.

"No," said Linnie, "I'm afraid I don't." She raised an
arm when she noticed me behind her and placed it over
my shoulders, pulling me in tight to her long grey skirt.

Mrs. Millar frowned and pointed at me with one
long, mauve fingernail.

"I don't know what you've been teaching her, but she just threatened to scalp my daughter."

Linnie wrinkled one eyebrow. "Don't be ridiculous. Shay has never even heard of such a thing, believe me."

"Well, that's what she told Margaret she'd do. Margaret just came home terribly upset."

Linnie looked down at me and stroked my hair.

"Is that what you said?"

"No, I said I hoped her hair would burn off."

Mrs. Millar made a sound of disapproval and drew in her chin. She smoothed her skirt and pinned her hands to her hips.

"Well, it's clear to me," she said, "that there's not much that can be done with these children. I thought you had some discretion in keeping her out of school, but now I don't know." Her eyelids, painted a faint purple, lowered a little. "Although I understand you can't have children of your own."

Linnie opened her mouth, then looked at me. "That's right." Her face set. "How kind of you to point it out, Mrs. Millar." She took a step backwards and I scurried back to keep pace.

"Goodbye," said Linnie, closing the door. Mrs. Millar's indignant face disappeared. Linnie turned and stroked my hair, her fingers fluttering a little as they reached the base of my neck.

"You and Mim got into a fight?" she asked, turning me by my shoulders to face her. She didn't sound upset. "I'm surprised it never happened before." She looked at me closely. "What was it about?"

"Does Mim's mother know that I'm adopted?"

Linnie's mouth twitched up. "Yes, honey."

"Does that mean that Mim knows that I'm adopted?" My chest felt tight and I was scared I was going to cry.

Linnie voice was gentle. "Honey," she said. "Everyone knows you're adopted."

"How do they know? Did you tell them?"

My mother sighed. "They can just tell because we don't look alike."

Then she returned to the sofa where she fell back asleep.

I CLIMBED THE STAIRS, GRIPPING HARD on the handrail. Once the bathroom door clicked shut behind me, I was startled by a deep sigh until I realized it had come from me. I locked the door and stood in front of the mirror.

"Emma," I whispered, "please tell me what to do." I was panting, with the same feeling in my chest that I got after running the whole length of our block and back. My whole face ached, too, with the effort of trying not to cry.

"When I open my eyes," I said, "you'll be standing behind me and we can have a conversation in the mirror."

When I next looked, it was still only me, and I could see that tears had begun leaking out the corners of my eyes while they were closed. I stared at the whites of my irises until my heart jumped and more tears spilled out. Then I wiped my face and noticed the pinkness of my palm against the contrast of my cheek and the colour of my arm, both almost the shade of the mirror's grainy light-walnut frame.

I stretched both arms out in front of me and gasped. I thought of the monkey in one of my favourite picture books. It was true what Linnie had said. I looked about as much like as her as Curious George looked like the Man in the Yellow Hat. My lips trembled, and I thought of Linnie's delicate smile, so frequent even in her deep sorrow. I gave up trying not to cry and sat down on the edge of the toilet seat.

There had always been something. I knew there had always been something that made me different from Linnie and Mim, different enough so that I could never look just like Shirley Temple or anyone out of the movies or the illustrations in any of my books. And I had always thought it was just that I was little less pretty and less grown up. But my dress, Emma's dress, could never really change anything. And there was no way to hide.

WE SAT IN THE KITCHEN before a late breakfast that Linnie said we would call brunch. She had slept in again, and I'd spent the first hour of the morning reading the book of the saints. I wondered if it was only through the grace of God that St. Alexius had been able to fool his parents into thinking he was someone else.

Garek was in his study, doing what he said was very important work that was sure to become trifling when the bacon was ready. In the afternoon light from the patio doors, Linnie's face seemed to be changing: it was brighter, almost luminous in the creases, but there were traces of lilac and cornflower blue in the hollows around her eyes, from her brow to her cheekbones. The radio was on. It was a children's choir, the clear sound of the hymn like a hundred flutes piping in harmony. My mother closed her eyes, her hands clasped around the sides of her mug.

"What beautiful voices," she said. She pushed her cup away and stood up.

Then she fell down.

For a moment, nothing seemed to happen. Linnie

was on the floor and I waited for her to get up. I might even have laughed, because her collapse was so abrupt that it was almost like slapstick, her face draining of all colour and expression before her legs crumpled just like an accordion, like Wile E. Coyote falling through the ground when the Road Runner hands him an anvil. But as I stood waiting for the world to restart, I must have made some noise, for Garek came downstairs and started yelling when he saw us.

"What happened?" he asked me. He kept hollering it over and over as he kneeled down beside Linnie, his hands cupping her face. I tried to tell him that I didn't know, but when I opened my mouth to speak I started crying. Then Garek put his ear over Linnie's mouth and was quiet, and when he stood up, he took two fast steps to the phone and called the ambulance, his voice too loud as he repeated our address into the receiver.

The minutes before the ambulance arrived were slow and panicky, and I dreamed them so often afterward I can no longer be sure which details I really remember and which ones I added in later. There was Garek beside Linnie on the floor, holding her and saying her name, and there was the feeling of cold from the tile seeping up through my socks and the sensation of floating away, farther and farther from both my parents. And there was

Garek looking up at me, with what I thought was blame, and then I smelled the porridge burning and I went to the stove and turned it off. I remember this because I had never touched the stove before, because Linnie had told me not to.

When I heard the siren, I fled to the living room and opened the door. I stepped back in the shadows as two men brought a stretcher down the hallway to the kitchen in a racket of noise almost enough to drown out Garek's shouts. Tiptoeing after them, I peeked around the edge of the doorway, keeping out of sight. Linnie's face was slack, and she looked as white and fragile as the tiny seashells Mrs. Gavranovic had lined up in a row on top of her television. Her hair was loose and strands of it lay crosswise upon her face in a way that, had she been awake, would have made her nose twitch until she brushed them away. I wanted to go to her and fix her hair and rub my hand along her arm, which was draped across her chest and looking thinner in its stillness. But she looked so small lying there, her legs barely a lump under the spreading folds of her blue skirt, that I was afraid to move. I watched her as hard as I could, as though I could keep her safe just by looking.

One of the men from the ambulance was trying to talk to Garek, while the other man spoke loudly to

Linnie as though she were deaf and touched the inside of her wrist. I thought I saw her eyelids flutter, as fast as blurring hummingbird wings, but the man shook his head and began pinching her middle finger just above the nail. Then he straightened and lifted her legs, and I flinched as her skirt began to slide up toward her waist, revealing her thin, pale thighs and white underwear. Garek was talking to the other man and didn't seem to notice. The man who was asking Garek questions had big, rounded shoulders. He peered down at Linnie's face, then bent at the knee to help lift her.

"Is she on any medication?" he asked. His face was blank as he turned to Garek for the answer, but his eyes were dark and active, and his hands were still supporting Linnie's head.

"Thorazine." Garek stepped forward to grab Linnie's limp hand within his own.

"Depressed?" asked the ambulance man. "Psychotic?" He held the wheeled stretcher steady as his partner buckled Linnie in. "Did she try to take her own life?"

"No," said Garek. "No. Migraines."

The man nodded and grabbed hold of the stretcher. I ran outside. Our house and the rest of our street looked normal, as if nothing bad had happened. There was a slight breeze lifting the petals of the pansies, and I stared at them harder than ever before. Their dark butterfly hearts seemed as velvety and inviting as small, warm beds. I wished very hard to become tiny enough to be able to live in the garden, to stay there. I concentrated on pulling in all my muscles until even my breathing sounded funny to me.

The men rattled past with Linnie a few seconds later.

"You can't come," the bigger one said to Garek. "Follow us in your car." Then he saw me, crouched beside the front steps.

"Who are you?" he said. "Get on home."

His curt glance fell across my face toward the ground, and he gave a nod back toward the street that made me turn to see if there was someone yet smaller and more insignificant standing behind me, somebody who might be the real object of his casual contempt. As I looked back at him it struck me that he was ugly, for his mouth was curled and unfriendly and the corners of his heavy brow spanned out past the width of his cheekbones—but then it seemed to me as though his gaze already contained everything I could ever think of him, good or bad. I tried to move or speak, but I felt fixed and yet absent within his look, like a small stain first observed but then quickly forgotten.

He turned away while I was still huddled, open-mouthed, trying to work out what to say to him. Garek had his back to me, unlocking the car, and I thought then that he would leave without me, his wrinkled white shirt flapping untucked in his haste like a maiden's handkerchief farewell. He was halfway into the driver's seat before he hauled himself out, one hand on the roof, and ran back to find me, cursing my mute gawking but kissing my forehead as he picked me up. I looked for the ambulance man to witness our display of kinship, but the sound of the siren was already retreating.

There were later rejections, friends who turned on me or turned away and lovers who cheated and lied and then despised my forgiveness, but the sting of the paramedic's remark never faded. It only deepened and soured as I kept trying in so many ways to do as he told me. I wanted to go home, or find a home, or make a home where I would never be questioned again and where I could find no questions to ask.

But I said nothing to Garek as we drove off, past Mrs. Gavranovic's, past Mim's, to the hospital. At first we followed the ambulance, until we got stopped by a red light and Garek had to slam on the brakes. I felt bereft as I watched the ambulance speed off ahead down the street, for there was something comforting in being washed in the coloured glow of its lights, the volume of its siren drowning out the possibility of any real thought.

AT THE HOSPITAL, GAREK ASKED one of the nurses to watch me while I sat in the waiting room. She sat me in the corner of the room closest to the desk, away from an old man with dark glasses and a bad cough, and across from a young woman who was crying quietly, wiping her eyes with the sleeve of her purple sweater. The nurse gave me a copy of *Highlights for Children*.

"Just look at this, honey," she said, and I read it from front to back, trying not to lift my eyes from its tattered pages in case I might see somebody else who was sick. As the afternoon wore on, more and more people came, but I did not let myself look up. The image of Linnie's pale face pressed along the floor frightened me every time it returned, and I did not know what other kind of stricken and ghastly faces might arrive.

I was squinting at a puzzle page, trying to count the differences between two pictures that looked the same, when my eyes began to droop. I lay down along two of the black vinyl chairs, my cheek sticky where it rested against the cover of the old magazine. I went in and out of sleep in this squashed pose, though the constant noise of the waiting room, with its shuffling footsteps and the shifting breezes of swinging doors, was always with me. The reason I was there was always with me, too, for in all of my half-dreams I was looking for Linnie or Emma, sure that I would find them both dead. When Garek touched my shoulder, I woke with a start, my kicking legs sending a waiting-room chair scraping across the floor with a loud screech.

"For the love of God," somebody said. I heard the hacking cough of the man in the dark glasses.

"She woke up in the ambulance," Garek told me, reaching for my hand. His voice sounded hoarse, and his cheeks, usually as round as two sails in a full wind, were sunken and dry. He rubbed the side of his chin with his wrist and blinked as he looked past me at the other people in the waiting room, though he did not appear to notice them.

"She said the siren was so loud that there was no way for her to keep sleeping." He made a gesture with his shoulders that seemed to exhaust him. "They're going to keep her overnight to make sure everything is fine," he said, and sighed. "And we should get you some food." When he saw my face, he added, "She's going to be okay."

ON THE WAY HOME, a litter of folded road maps cascaded off the dashboard and onto my lap as Garek made a sharp turn. I looked at him as I pushed the maps to the car's dirty floor. He said nothing, but I saw that there were beads of sweat on the back of his neck. The maps lay there on the rubber mat, half-unfolded, just out of reach of my foot.

"I'll get them," I said, after a beat. "I'm sorry I dropped them." I reached to undo my seatbelt, but Garek stopped me, moving his hand to cover mine.

"Leave them," he said. "Please." Garek gripped the steering wheel again with both hands and I saw his shoulders tense up, then relax. "Please," he repeated.

"Okay," I said.

We drove in silence, a little slower, with Garek sometimes shaking his head as he breathed loud and deep through his nose.

"Is Mummy going to die?" I asked. I watched his face, staring hard at his white, chapped lips.

"No, I told you. She just fainted. She's going to be fine." He looked over at me, pressing his lips together into something that was not quite a smile. His voice had the rougher edge that it had when he was upset, but I knew he wasn't angry. "It's like sleeping."

The drive could not have been very long, but it seemed to go in and out like this, with Garek speeding off and on, sometimes speaking, sometimes not. As we drove, Garek pointed out the canal and the river, and the spot where, down the road, the city would meet the country, and where that road would lead on to other cities, to places I had never been before.

"You've been along this road before," he said. "As a baby."

"Was I a pretty baby?" It was a phrase I had heard used to describe babies before, mostly by Mrs. Gavranovic in reference to long-ago generations of her family, befrilled and elongated in christening gowns in aging photographs. I was never convinced of the beauty she claimed for those bunched and complaining little faces, and I watched Garek's eyes as he drove, as they flickered from me to the road. I was surprised when he didn't hesitate.

"Oh, yes," he said. "Very lovely eyes, and very attentive, too, right from the beginning." He sounded tired. He gave me a brief smile before looking back to the road. A driver honked his horn and Garek rolled his eyes.

"Am I an Indian?" I asked. "Am I like those kids that you take out of the forest?"

I saw the large knuckles of his hands tighten against the steering wheel.

"No," he said. Then, "Yes." Then he looked straight ahead at the road and did not say anything else.

I looked out the window. The imperfections in the

asphalt blurred as we merged, picking up speed, onto the Queensway. I turned my hands over and over in my lap. When I grabbed hold of the dashboard, wanting something to cling to, Garek turned on the radio, and I let go. As I squinted into the sun, the broken white line dividing the highway became a solid streak, and I tracked it until it was blocked from view by the cars up ahead, each as big and as bright as the spots of colour I saw when I closed my eyes.

Acknowledgements

VERSIONS OF THESE STORIES have previously appeared in literary journals: "Mother Superior" in *PRISM international*, "Look, But Don't Touch" in *Grain*, "My Three Girls" in *Prairie Fire*, "Bloodlines" in *The New Quarterly*, and "Scar Tissue" in *The Dalhousie Review*. Many thanks to the editors of these journals for the opportunities and encouragement that these acceptances provided.

I gratefully acknowledge the Manitoba Arts Council and the University of Manitoba Graduate Fellowships for providing financial support at the beginning of this project, the Conseil des arts et des lettres du Québec for supporting me through the end, and the Department of Philosophy at McGill University for employing me in the meantime.

Many thanks to the Banff Centre and to Edna Alford for being a generous and discerning reader, and to Warren Cariou for much help and critical encouragement. Thanks also to Jonathan Ball and Alice Zorn for perceptive readings of "The Republic of Rose Island."

I am especially indebted to my editor, Melanie Little, for her faith and insight. I am forever grateful.

Finally, profound thanks to my mother and to all my friends and family. Special thanks to Bob Kotyk, for everything, and to his family, too, for their amazing kindness and warmth.

➔

Saleema Nawaz's fiction has appeared in journals including *Prairie Fire*, *Grain*, *The New Quarterly*, and *PRISM international* and she is an alumnus of the Writing Studio at the Banff Centre for the Arts. "The White Dress," the final novella in this book, won the inaugural Robert Kroetsch Award for Best Creative Thesis at the University of Manitoba. She lives in Montreal, where she is at work on her first novel.